Philip's Girl

PHILIP'S GIRL

LUCY FERRISS

Schocken Books   New York

First published by Schocken Books 1985

10 9 8 7 6 5 4 3 2 1   85 86 87 88

Copyright © 1985 Lucy Ferriss

Library of Congress Cataloging in Publication Data
Ferriss, Lucy, 1954–
Philip's girl.
I. Title.
PS3556.E754P5   1985   813'.54   84–22226

Designed by Jane Byers Bierhorst
Manufactured in the United States of America
ISBN 0–8052–3976–6

FOR MARK

Philip's Girl

Chapter 1

PERIHELION

Philip Decker was mildly famous. Mildly because no one involved in something so purely academic as philosophy of mind
could become a household word unless he committed an outrage
or went political. But the nature of his fame had led everyone to
think he must be brilliant as well, and then to wonder why he was
not more famous than he was.

The basis for Philip's fame was a series of books, almost identi-
cally printed and bound, though the publisher had put a different
brightly colored dustjacket on each one. *The Language of Perception, The Biology of Thought, Physical Parapsychology, Vitalism:* red,

yellow, green, blue. He lectured not only to academicians but to doctors, brain researchers, psychiatrists, mystics. When one young scientist confessed on meeting him that he had thought Philip Decker was already dead, Philip felt assured of a few years of posthumous recognition.

They were comforting in a small way, the recognition and the money. He used the money to travel, mostly, and to take leaves without pay, and sometimes he gambled it away in Las Vegas. He liked Las Vegas, its mystery and its danger—he could step back, like a true skeptic, and observe in himself the urge to risk all, to play with fate. Otherwise he thought little about the books—they were written and done with. For years he turned down offers from prestigious universities in the East, some with substantial salaries attached. He didn't like people to expect too much of him, because he knew that he was not in fact brilliant, only knowledgeable and sharp, and he suspected that soon he might have nothing left to say. Also he didn't want to move his family—Joan and the two girls—and he enjoyed the small college and the sunny town—or he had, when the offers had been coming in. Now that they'd stopped he got irritated with it all sometimes. But he used to be almost content with his family and his work, and he would smile benignly on those who thought him an unhappy man. Then he had begun, at some untraceable point, to want something more. Something more, that was all—a richer life, a wider capacity for intimacy than marriage afforded. And he was sure when he began to want it that even if he never found it, no great harm would be done.

It was after fifteen steady years of marriage to Joan that Philip began seeing other women. The first girl's name was Linda, and she was a tough, sexy undergraduate who had a reputation for liking to fuck professors. She was taking two of his classes and used to hang around his office afterward, her hands shoved neatly into the back pockets of her jeans so that her breasts thrust themselves at him. Finally she had invited him to a party at her place, and to his own surprise he had gone, telling Joan it was a department meeting. Linda had received him at the door in a black jersey and tight black pants with silver brads running down her hips, and she had escorted him past the crowd of pot-smoking students. He had made a pass at her before he left. She stood against the wall in the back room and tugged on his kisses, her mouth wide and loose. His hands were on the wall, hers hung at her sides; but as he pressed his body against hers he felt her push back, insistent. He left then. He was not given to impulse, and something in the girl, in her calculated abandon, frightened him. But he came back the next night, when she was alone.

Remembering Linda with fondness, he returned to his old life for a few months after she graduated. Then he met a psychologist at a conference; then there was an art student; then a doctor. It was rarely exciting anymore, but it was often satisfying, and he liked the women very much. They were good to him as he was to them, and they all lived by a code that left him free. But of course he had to lie to Joan, and he had to meet his lovers in secret, and while he knew this was necessary, he could not believe it was right. It irked him, to lie. He imagined Joan finding him out, and the uselessness of his only defense: "Whom have I hurt? There was nothing lacking in you. I only wanted more." And he found that the women gave him something more, though not enough— less, in fact, each time. The affairs became just one way to stem the vexation of spirit that gnawed at his daily life and at his work. When they failed, he picked up the handy tool of his skepticism and regarded himself as an example of the biological blunder that was man, rooted in guilt, plagued by desires and limitations, and afraid of death.

He thought sometimes that his elder daughter, Didi, understood him, and while this didn't matter, it gave him pleasure. When she was young he used to take her fishing, and they would sit there for hours together in the boat without exchanging a word. At first she had wanted to throw the fish back; she felt sorry for them, she said. But he had explained the unwritten rule of the sport: if you didn't keep the fish you caught, and eat them, you weren't really fishing. He believed that.

Didi was never clever or gifted, but she was wise early, with round eyes that regarded the world as if they saw through its surface. She laughed a lot and made him laugh, and spending time with her simplified things greatly. They caught buckets of pewtery bass and perch, and Didi cleaned them carefully, asking about the bones and the entrails and the fishes' habits.

He was sorry when Didi found out about Linda, and he also wished in his vanity that it had been a different woman. He lied and promised there were no others, but by then it didn't matter. Whatever had broken was permanently broken, and reflected in his daughter's eyes he saw his own guilt and unrest. He was glad when she went away to college. When she came home on vacation, blooming and excited and distant with the novelty of separation, he was wary of her, and awkward when they were alone. She didn't mind the infidelity to her mother, he knew that—*But you should have told me,* her eyes said, and whenever he was seeing a woman while she was home, her look seemed to say *You should tell me.* He didn't—no reason to, a thousand reasons not to. Still she lay in wait, demanding, making him edgy. But everything else was frank and open between them, so that when she would leave, he would decide he had imagined the silent reproach.

The summer of Didi's nineteenth birthday, Philip took her canoeing down the Colorado with Jack Wheelbright and Jack's girlfriend, Ruth. Joan had work to do and elected to stay home with six-year-old Emily. Out on the river Philip and Didi could enjoy a glorious freedom together, in spite of the August heat and Jack, who complained nightly about his sore hands and wet clothes.

When Jack first came to Newhall College, Philip had welcomed a new face, and they had spent a lot of time together. They would drink and discuss heady ideas late into the night. Jack had been a precocious student, an existentialist, fashionable at the time. Now he was thirty-three and already had tenure, and he had become prematurely stale and riddled with pedantic anxieties.

Didi had never looked healthier, Philip remembered later. He thought she must have been at that peak young women reach at some point between sixteen and twenty-five—though she reminded him more of himself as a young man than of any women he knew. She had inherited none of her mother's frail prettiness, Joan's watery skin or gossamer features. Tall, large-boned, handsome in a genial sort of way, Didi was like himself, as he had been once. It alway surprised Philip when boys were attracted to his daughter. When she flirted with them, he studied her easy sexuality, as if trying to decipher a code. But then sometimes she would ignore men altogether, as on this float trip, when she attached herself to Ruth, not whispering with her at odd moments like most women but speaking directly to her in the course of conversation, caring most about what Ruth said. Ruth was black and taught psychology at the Black Studies Center, and Didi asked her sudden questions about what it was like—to grow up in Watts, to teach at such a honky college, to have a white lover. Jack was baffled—a little jealous, even. He finally asked, with everyone around the fire one night, drinking, why Didi was so damn interested in Ruth. The two women looked at him, startled as if out of a dream. Then Didi said she liked Ruth, that's why, didn't Jack like her? And Ruth echoed that she liked Didi, and started to question her about things too—but something was lost. Their speech after that moment sounded artificial.

Philip found himself studying Didi like a strange species as they went down the river, like one of those alien shore birds he used to be given when the lab class was told to identify habits, adaptations, habitat, and food by the shape and size of the bill and wings and feathers and guts. He looked for clues, for signals, when Didi started a paddle-splashing fight with the other canoe or when she disappeared once, going off into the woods by herself before dawn.

Or maybe it was a study of himself he was making. He recognized everything she did—it was all familiar. But it was like observing a pattern without knowing its underlying principle; he simply couldn't piece it together. Tired of being a teacher, he wanted to learn again. And none of the women he found seemed to teach him anything anymore, so he was looking.

On the fourth and last day of the trip, during the chill early morning, Jack maneuvered his canoe into a breach and tipped. The current over the rocks was so loud that the first sign Didi and Philip had of the accident was the bright red pack that went swirling past their canoe in the clear water. Next came a paddle and then Jack, holding on to the keel of his canoe and grabbing the stern of theirs. They let the pack go but got the paddle and the sleeping bags that followed. Ruth was hanging on to the growth of the bank upstream, and after hoisting her in, they drifted to a sand bar. Ruth's shoulder was injured—a sprain, Philip thought, but Didi was the one who touched it cautiously and moved it and asked when it hurt. She gave Ruth her dry clothes and sat talking to her while the men emptied the water out of the canoe.

As he watched Didi sitting on a log next to Ruth, Philip wanted to step into one or the other of their bodies, to achieve whatever accord they had together that he'd lost with his daughter and found nowhere else. A language already agreed upon ran underneath the words they used, and the words seemed to touch.

Newhall College didn't resume classes until the end of September. Through the summer, the smog had drifted north from Los Angeles in its usual path, seeping past the Simi Valley into the foothills of the San Rafaels, where the town lay in a pocket. But by October, when Didi had left for school, the air had cleared to where you could see the mountains again. It was then, as the odd deciduous trees, planted by New Englanders who had founded the college, had begun to litter the street with dead leaves, that Philip met Annie Redfield.

"Met" wasn't the right word. She was finishing her major in philosophy, though no one quite knew why she had chosen that field; and he had taught her in a class on existentialism the year before, when Jack Wheelbright was on leave. Philip didn't like the existentialists—their concepts were murky to him, and he distrusted murk. He remembered Annie Redfield because she had understood the muddle of material better than he did, even though she couldn't use a strand of logic. Her crowd seemed to

be the theater and art students, and as he grew curious he learned
that she had a job with the drama department, designing costumes. He had noticed her clothing, last year—she sprinkled her
jeans outfits with short capes and quilted vests and cinched her
loose dresses with bright woven belts, tied tight on her thin waist
or hanging over her hips. She had a certain appealing awkwardness—the clothes never quite fit. Intellectually she reminded him
of the small covey of bright women in his regular classes who
argued with clear and articulate voices, showing up the myopic
and unformed men beside them; but unlike those women she
would suddenly retreat, after her impassioned explanations of
Sartre, and shrink into herself as if embarrassed. The only one in
the department who knew her personally was Jack, who had
pursued her when she first arrived at Newhall three years ago.
She had put Jack off with an unaffected eighteen-year-old innocence, but he still took her to lunch, and Philip had seen him
coming down from the costume shop where Annie worked.

That was all Philip knew in October, when Annie Redfield
made an appointment to see him and discuss the possibility that
he might advise her on her thesis. "I've got a group of essays,"
she said on the phone. "One that I wrote for your class, and a
couple of others. If you'll read them, I'm sure you'll see what I'm
driving at."

"They aren't about Nothingness, are they?"

"No. No, really they're about something."

"Okay, then, bring them by."

When she came to his office Annie sat in the stiff metal chair in
front of Philip's desk instead of the more comfortable one farther
back. She looked anxiously at her papers on his blotter and at his
notes, and she waited for him to begin some kind of discussion.
The boldness of the classroom had left her, shed like an extra
skin. Ill at ease as they began to talk, she kept fiddling with the
buttons on her leather vest. He joked with her about the existentialism class, then he honed in on what she was writing, which
had something to do with perception and art. Eventually she
leaned back in the chair and left the vest alone, and she brought

forth some of her ideas, which weren't bad once he got them clear, though he couldn't tell at first whether she needed help in expressing her thoughts or in thinking them through.

But he could tell something. For the first time he thought he could hear the language underneath the words, the language he'd always spoken but never understood. It lay in her slim body and fine-textured skin; it moved in her eyes and in the hands that continually gestured while she spoke. He wanted to take hold of it, but he also wanted it to go away. The sensation wasn't just desire—he was used to that. It was a connection, something more central and more hazardous.

Philip stayed home a lot of those first weeks, out of defense and out of preparation. He worked on his new book, *The Matter of the Soul;* caught up on correspondence; wrote Didi. He played with Emily and tried to make something more of the family. He talked to Joan about the possibility of taking a leave the next year, maybe going back to England, where they had spent six months after his first book came out. But there would still be a year, and he still wanted something he couldn't elude, which hovered over him like an insistent breath of wind: he was going to have her.

◇   ◇   ◇   ◇   ◇   ◇   ◇   ◇   ◇

"I don't think I could choose a major where you had to write a thesis," said Annie's friend Mona, trying on a cloche hat in the costume studio.

"I'm hoping it'll teach me to think," Annie said. "Hand me that bit of interfacing, will you? I can't move from this machine."

"I wish you could finish up. Clyde starts his film in twenty minutes, and he's always on time."

"Go on by yourself, then. I don't mind."

"*I* do. I'll be bored. You don't want to spend the whole week in this firetrap, do you?"

Annie shrugged. "I was at a philosophy shindig last night," she said. "And this has to be ready for rehearsal tomorrow."

"Was the professor there?" Mona leaned across the sewing table and caught Annie's eye.

"If you mean Philip Decker, yes. With his wife. They left early."

"Is it still—well, *awkward?*" Mona hung up the cloche and took a bowler. Without waiting for Annie to answer, she went on, "I should think it must be. I remember when Bruce was first interested in me, back at Wellesley. The power he wielded! Of course that was different, there was a chemistry between us. You're not actually interested in this man, are you?"

"I don't know." Annie pulled the dress she was making out of the machine and, leaning back in the wooden folding chair, pushed her fine, curly hair back from her face. She looked small in the chair, surrounded by yards of blue velvet, though in fact she stood taller than Mona, who had cast the bowler aside and was turning in front of the mirror with a tam pulled low on her forehead. For Mona to suggest she not be interested implied immediately that the person was not worth any interest. "I'm really not the type. I was so amazed Halloween night—when he—"

"Made a pass at you?"

"Yeah."

"I don't know why you should be. You've had that other one—Jack?"

"Wheelbright. Right."

"He's been after you for years, you tell me. But God, Annie, you better handle it right. Bruce just overwhelmed me. The lies, the deception! His wife, the school, my parents, my friends, his wife some more. I was eighteen, Annie, can you believe it?"

"I remember when you first came to Newhall, this married student," Annie said, folding the velvet. "I thought you were terribly old and mysterious, showing up at plays with this balding husband from the East Coast. Even when we got to be friends, you never talked about him. Then bam! One day you plunk down in the middle of a workshop and announce you're divorcing him. That hat looks good on you."

"It was the happiest day of my life!" Mona had put the bowler back on and was tucking her hair under its brim. "Just to be with people my own age again, not to mention everything that was wrong with Bruce." She adjusted the hat and shook her head. "I don't want you hurt. These men don't sound good for you."

"I have to think what to do about my thesis. Find out if he's read my essays. I'm embarrassed to go talk to him."

"You're embarrassed? *He's* the one who made the pass. You've got to go out more. Get a perspective on this. Not that I know who you'd go out with. I haven't seen a less attractive group *anywhere*. Don't you think, on the whole? They're all hairy and skinny, and *short*. Short men, everywhere you look."

"Not Clyde."

"But even Clyde's gawky. I just forget because he attracts me. There's that Dave person I've seen you with. Why aren't you closer to him?"

Annie shrugged. She had no answers to give Mona, for whom passion had always been an inevitable weakness. She could not explain to her friend that she had to wait, still and expectant, for passion to call to her. "He hasn't asked me," she said. "There, I'm done. Let's go."

Annie locked the wardrobe and shut the lights. The two women descended the long, straight staircase, which ran the length of the theater to the backstage, and emerged in late-afternoon light on the walk behind the building, where beds of ivy shot their tendrils up to claw at the fabric of the wall. "I heard from Bruce today," said Mona.

"And?"

"He wants my half of the double sleeping bag. For Judy, I imagine. I said no. So he of course said what's the use of it being a double sleeping bag if you don't have both halves, which is very practical but a little beside the emotional point."

"You gave in?"

"I gave in."

Mona, who had married Bruce when she was nineteen and divorced him when she was twenty-one, had been an anomaly when she first came to join the bright, energetic students at Newhall. Annie had fallen in with her because she had felt herself out of place—the studio full of fanciful costumes her only domain, other students shying away, while professors like Jack Wheelbright zeroed in on her as if she shared some secret with them. As soon as she met Mona she had known there could be no replacement—it would be Mona's secrets she shared, Mona to whom she confessed. Only what had happened at Halloween had challenged that.

"Between us," Mona said to Annie as they walked to the Union where Clyde was showing his film, "we could make the perfect woman. Don't you think?"

"Well, there's your hair," Annie said, glancing as a breeze blew it back from Mona's shoulders.

"Your bone structure."

"I guess my cheeks are better. Your skin."

"Maybe. Definitely my eyes."

"You think so?" Annie met Mona's large brown eyes, the pale lashes arching away from the edges like a grace note, the brows curving prettily above. Her own—deep-set, bright blue flecked with gold—had an Irish flash from her mother; the brows above were long and heavy. Her best feature. "Okay, yours," she conceded to Mona.

"Neither of our noses."

"Perfect woman has to have a nose. Mine's too pointy."

"All right, but your mouth. My upper lip stinks."

"I've never liked my mouth. It's too full."

"So? That's sensual. It has to be your mouth."

They traveled down their bodies—Annie's long neck, Mona's shoulders and breasts, Annie's ass and legs, Mona's small and graceful feet. "You can't take too much of me below the neck until I lose a few pounds," Mona said. "Tennis this fall."

"Great. Early mornings, we can get a court."

Clyde's film was a study of Mona's feet as they ran through leaves on the quad, scaled a tree, pointed and stretched in the air. Mona and Annie sat in the back and whispered until Clyde turned and frowned at them. In the darkness of the film room, in the muddle of her confusion over Philip Decker, Annie felt suddenly grateful. Mona was beautiful and mysterious and lonely, and Annie was sane and lonely and understood her. In their isolation they had sifted their lives through each other as if they could filter out some premature wisdom. Any impending moment could rupture the bond, and so Annie was grateful, in the dark, for each moment of charmed stasis, each abeyance.

◇   ◇   ◇   ◇   ◇   ◇   ◇   ◇   ◇

A week later, Annie was sipping coffee as she waited for Philip Decker on the side porch of the student union. The morning sun was strong, for November, and she squinted up at it as she stretched her arms. The heat relaxed her and seemed to quiet the shaking in her arms and legs. She was hungry. Nerves always made her hungry, and then it made her both nervous and self-conscious to feel she was eating too much. So she sipped at the black coffee and rolled up the blousy sleeves of her dress and tried to focus her thoughts on the papers Philip would be bringing with him.

She had called the department, finally, to make the appointment. If Philip Decker wasn't going to act as her thesis adviser after all, she needed to know quickly. He had left word that he would meet her, on the terrace, at eleven. It would be the first time they had spoken since that Halloween night, when he had helped her carry plates home from a college party and kissed her in the doorway of her kitchen. She knew now that she should have expected that; she knew, too, that she had brought it on. What she had not known—what she still did not know—was what to do about it. She had pushed him away, then. He had said, "Another time," and left. Now she would do something else—she was preparing to do something else. But she did not understand what it was.

Let him come soon, she thought, and suddenly there he was, blotting out the glare of the sun.

"Getting a tan in November?" he asked.

"Someone told me the sun was actually closer to the earth in the winter."

"Perihelion, yes. But it's too far south to do you any good. The atmosphere blocks the ultraviolet."

"It warms my bones, anyhow." This was going to be easy, Annie realized. Philip pulled up a chair and sat with his back to the sun. There was no awkwardness, no embarrassment. She needed no stock of little jokes. And he still liked her.

"I've looked over your essays," Philip said, laying a folder marked "Annie Redfield" on the table. "I'm not sure I understand what you're trying to do."

"I want to explain a different way of seeing."

"There are dozens of ways of seeing. Which one are you after? Frankly, I can't tell by what you've written here."

What I see when I sketch, Annie wanted to say, but it didn't sound very philosophical. "The artistic way," she tried. "The type of perception that leads someone to create something."

"You mean like aesthetic contemplation."

"No, I mean a different way of looking at the world. It might be very active. It needn't take place in a museum—it probably doesn't."

"This is really a thesis on aesthetics, Annie. You should be working with Jack Wheelbright."

"I'd thought of that, but he's . . . well, I'd rather not." Philip grinned. She wouldn't have to explain about Jack. "Besides, what I really want to talk about is a certain way the mind works. That's your field, isn't it? I want to bring in things like depth. Like time and space. The way a single motion will arrest the eye. Aestheticians talk about beauty. I don't want to talk about beauty."

"Well, okay then, I'm happy to work with you. But the first thing you have to do is stop asking questions. You have three pages here of nothing but questions. That won't get you anywhere. Then you have two more pages where you 'define your terms.' That won't help either. You've got to start writing—just putting down what you think on paper, as clearly and simply as you can. And I'll assign you some reading material, just to give you an idea of different approaches. Write these down. . . ."

As the sun rose higher, Philip moved his chair into the shade. Classes had broken, and students milled around them, but to Annie the other people seemed far away. Out of the corner of her eye she saw Urban Whittaker, the department head, lean his heavy body on the railing as he came up the steps to join them. When he reached the top he stopped and stood scratching his short, stubbly beard. After a minute he turned into the Union, leaving them alone. As the stream of people flowed by, Annie forgot that she was afraid of Philip. He was listening to her, and he was talking to her, and ideas filled the space around them, and there was nothing else except the cold coffee and her notes and the brilliant sun.

"Well, I guess that does it," Philip said finally.

"I should say! This could be enough reading for a dissertation."

"They're just suggestions, remember."

"But I'll feel like an idiot if I don't at least check them out. Especially this book *you* wrote. I've got to cover myself."

Philip leaned back in his chair and rubbed his hands over his face. Annie looked at the clock on the tower. She drew one long breath and thought, *Now.* "It's almost noon," she said. "How about lunch?"

Philip took his hands away from his face and squinted at her. "Terrific," he said. "Your car or mine?"

"Yours. I don't have a car."

The interior of the restaurant was decorated to resemble a prewar railway car, with deep-red wallpaper and tiny booths. To Annie it felt perfect. The waitress brought them drinks—his a gin martini straight up, her an old-fashioned, too sweet. Since Philip wasn't looking at the menu, Annie didn't either. He lit a cigarette, and in the dim light filtering through its smoke they each leaned back against the red leather cushions, their hands caressing the liquor glasses that caught the light before them. A couple of Philip's philosophy jokes made them laugh, awkwardly, and then Annie lit a cigarette too. When they had to give an order, she took the first thing she saw on the menu, cream of mushroom soup and a salad. He had a steak sandwich. Everything seemed to happen in slow motion, each detail a small painting. The waitress brought them more drinks, then some wine that Philip chose.

They talked about careers. Philip said he had once planned to be a doctor.

"What happened?"

"I saw my first cadaver. I was in medical school, and when they got to cadavers I just turned and walked out."

"And went into philosophy."

"And went into the navy, then philosophy."

He was stationed in Panama, he said, during the Korean War. At night it was his duty to go ashore, prowl the red-light district, comb through the houses for sailors, and get them back onto the ship. Annie said she thought that would be an unpopular job, but he said he always gave them time to finish before he hauled them out.

"I was just there a year. I contracted mild hepatitis and got a medical discharge in the spring. By fall I was well and entered Columbia on the G.I. Bill."

"Oh, so that was the point of the navy."

"Well, it did help."

Annie buttered bread as they talked, and nibbled at the salad. "It's funny," Philip went on. "I've never been confused about what I wanted to do. I've changed my mind, but things have always been clear. I think it's different for kids today."

Kids, thought Annie.

He said he had met Joan in New York and married her. They had come out to the Coast the next year.

Laughing about the sailors again, Annie and Philip finished the wine and split the check. Outside the sun shone, a reproach, hurting their eyes. "Where to?" he asked.

"Home, I guess. If it's not out of your way."

"Not at all."

When he parked the car by her place, the street was deserted. He turned off the engine, and as if by reflex Annie asked if he

would like coffee. Of course he said he would. Of course, because he could not have refused, and the alcohol had washed
away all awkwardness. Annie couldn't arrest the perfect timing,
or alter the smooth inflection with which she spoke. As she
unlocked the door she remembered she had cleaned the apartment that morning and bought wine and beer at the market—
hiding this possibility all the while, refusing to anticipate it. She
smiled at herself.

"What's funny?"

"Nothing. I'll tell you sometime."

He preferred beer to coffee. She opened two cans and sat on
the single bed, leaving him the only chair, a frayed green recliner
she had found in the garage. He didn't sit down but walked
around the room, and she grew nervous again. "It's strictly Salva-
tion Army," she said. "I didn't see the point in anything more
when I don't know where I'll be in eight months."

"Oh, no, you've done a good job." He grinned. "I think they
call it Camp." He glanced at her sketches for costumes, tacked up
on two walls. "You did these?"

"Uh-huh."

"They're quite good."

"Thanks."

Philip came over to the bed and looked out the window.
"That's a huge oak, all right," he said.

"That's not an oak."

"Sure it is."

"It's an evergreen. It doesn't have acorns."

"It's a California live oak—the acorns are very small. It's not a
tree you'd have seen, growing up in Michigan."

Three years I've been here, Annie thought, and I never knew
that. As much as anything, it mattered that he find her intelligent.
What a stupid thing not to know.

But he had turned and was standing in front of her. He put his
beer on the windowsill, leaned down, and kissed her forehead.
She couldn't look up at him, but she reached her arms around his

neck, and he sank to his knees by the bed. "I don't know if you remember," he said, "a couple of weeks ago—"

"I remember. I told you to leave."

"But you won't make me leave now?"

"No."

He kissed her breasts and reached a hand under the thin skirt of her dress. "Did you think I would take you up on it?" she said to the top of his head. The hair there was thinning.

"It wasn't if, it was when." He untied the sash around her waist and moved both hands under the skirt, to her hips. Then he stood up, lifting her up with him, against him, and her dress floated over her head. He sat on the bed and she stood dumbly, watching him undress. Only when he was done did she slip out of her panties and sit by him. He pulled the covers off the bed and laid her down on the sheet. Kneeling between her thighs, he put her legs around his waist, and as his hands traveled over her hips and waist and onto her breasts he whispered, "Christ, you're lovely." But Annie hardly heard him, so loud was the pounding of blood in her ears, and tightening her calves she pulled him to her.

They sat on the floor afterward, leaning against the bed, smoking and finishing the beers. He had dressed and combed his hair—Annie had watched his reflection in the mirror as he combed it back and smoothed it with his hand. She was in the kimono her father had brought back from Japan, a faded silk print with mandarin ducks. Philip touched her knee gingerly, as if examining it for a fracture. "We don't have to continue this, you know," he said.

"Oh, but let's." The words fell like water from her mouth. Her whole body was light, fluid.

"I'm a little afraid. You're very young—I don't want to be taking advantage of that."

"Nonsense. I'm a free woman—I do as I choose." She tapped the ash from her cigarette, and they both watched the ember miss the dish and expire on the rug.

"I know," Philip said. "But you can't fall in love with me."

"I know."

"So just don't. All right?"

She took hold of her toes, as if to rock herself. "Every man you sleep with you love a little bit," she said.

"You don't have to worry, by the way."

"Worry?"

"About pregnancy."

It took her a moment to comprehend him. "A vasectomy?"

"It doesn't affect my sex life."

"Obviously not." But of course: his family was complete.

They kissed for a long time at the door. His hand reached to her thigh and lifted her up against him. "When do I see you again?" he asked.

"In class tomorrow at eleven."

"I mean without your clothes."

"Thursday afternoon?"

"Fine."

"Around three."

"I'll be here."

He walked quickly down the steps to his car, glancing right and left as he went. Annie cleaned up the cans and ashes. It was perfect. *You are having an affair with Philip Decker,* she whispered to herself. *We are having an affair. He was here, he was with me, he will come back.* It was simple. It was that simple.

Next morning Annie woke to the telephone. She sat up straight at the first ring, then fumbled on the night stand for the receiver. It was Mona, waiting at the tennis courts.

"Sorry, I forgot," Annie said, pushing away the sheets. "Give me ten minutes, I'll be there."

"Okay. But we won't have much time to play. I've got a class."

"Five minutes."

Annie threw on a knit top and shorts, unscrewed her racquet

from its brace, and found the can of tennis balls she had bought the day before. Mona was waiting by the far court at the other end of the campus, her thick gold hair knotted into a bun and shining in the morning sun. She paced up and down the short walk, swinging her racquet through the cool air. In her peach-colored top and her jeans she looked soft and ripe, and when she came to meet Annie she moved as if buffeted by a secret fragrance.

"You're flushed," she said, touching Annie's cheek. "You're hot."

"I ran all the way down here."

"No, it's not just that. You never oversleep, either. Did you spend the night with someone?"

"No. Well, not exactly." Annie opened the new can, the pressured air sighing as she released it, and she sniffed the fresh tennis balls. She could tell one person at least. At least, she could tell Mona. "You remember Philip Decker."

"He's your thesis adviser. He's attracted to you."

"Yeah, well, I spent yesterday afternoon with him."

"You went to bed with him?" Annie nodded. Mona looked her up and down, as if she were seeing a strange and not altogether pleasant creature. "Did you like it?"

"It was wonderful."

"Are you going to keep seeing him?"

"I think so."

"He's a lot older than you are."

"I realize that."

"Well, I'm certainly not one to give you any advice."

"I don't think I need any, really. Everything's fine."

"But how did it happen? What brought it on?"

"We just had lunch together, and then I asked him over for coffee. Don't ask me why—I just did. It seemed right."

"I worry about you. I feel protective of you."

"Don't," Annie said, smiling. "Come on, let's play. You serve."

Mona's serve was strong but predictable; Annie returned the ball with a weak spin, then ran back to be ready for Mona's long shot. They were used to each other's game by now. There was even an emotional pattern to their playing. A good game meant they could face each other; the simple grace of movement and the fresh air freed them from their melodramas and cleared out hidden anger. A bad game left them dark, unwholesome. Mona would slam her racquet into the fence and yell, "I hate this stupid fucking game! I hate it!" or she would walk off the court in the middle of a point and sit under a tree and begin to cry. Players on the other courts would watch curiously as Annie gathered up the balls and told the couple waiting they could play now. The spring before, when Mona had been getting her divorce from Bruce, she would insist on playing tennis and then break down in the middle of a set.

Her three years with Bruce were Mona's constant subject. She re-created them with the neat horror of a tabloid, the characters smudged with mythic dirt. Bruce had been her teacher at a school in the East—"my mentor," Mona would say, as if the word meant "assassin." He had taught her to write poetry; he had taught her to have orgasms; he had taught her politics. His first wife, Iris, had been desperate when she found out, Mona said. He was everything to Iris too, and she had wanted to set up a ménage, the three of them together in the abandoned church Bruce had rebuilt into a house, with the bed where the altar had been. But he had divorced Iris and married Mona, and they had moved out here, where she had been surrounded by his brilliant, neurotic friends—all of them older, some famous—all of them into cocktail parties and analysis.

After tennis Mona and Annie would head for the gym to sweat in the sauna, or they would go out for a liter of wine, and Annie would sit rapt as a child before a gruesome fairy tale while Mona's voice went on like an oracle. But Annie had never rid herself of the uneasy feeling that something was being left out of Mona's story, as if all the talk wove a veil around the gap. The spring after they met, the two women would stay up until daybreak in Mona's house, signs of Bruce everywhere, talking and smoking the little cigars—Erics they were called, sometimes they substituted Tiparillos—which had distinguished them that year.

This fall, hooking up with twenty-year-old Clyde, Mona had returned vigorously to normality, and tennis had ceased to unnerve her. She was a better player than Annie; she had taken lessons and moved in perfect form. But Annie's game was fast and tricky, and today she felt strong. She won Mona's serve, then her own.

"Let's just play four out of seven," Mona said. "It's all I've got time for."

Threatened with defeat, Mona always improved her game. She served to Annie's backhand, then rushed the net and volleyed the return. The next two points she took by placing the ball carefully in the back corner, just missing the alley. Mona played best when she was angry or ecstatic; she seemed to enlarge, her skin hardened, and her arm came down over the ball in a sure, straight line for the serve. She was angry about something today, but while Annie noticed, she couldn't bring herself to ask about it. Annie played best when she wasn't thinking about the game or about Mona. When she moved in a kind of trance, focusing only on the ball, almost unconscious, her tennis improved.

"Clyde might move in with me!" Mona shouted over the net.

"What about his parents?"

"They won't know. There's a guy who wants to move into the dorm, and Clyde'll just tell them he's trading places with him in a house off campus. They won't be out here until graduation anyway."

"Are you sure you want to live with somebody? So soon after Bruce, I mean."

"Annie, I've never been so sure of anything in my whole life." Mona paused in her serve and came up to the net. "There just aren't any problems when Clyde and I are together. It's the opposite of being married to Bruce. It's tender. It's innocent. And we're together all the time anyway, so it won't really make much difference."

Clyde was collegiate as a football, and Mona adored him. She was a theater major now, having dropped English shortly after she dropped Bruce, and she had persuaded Clyde to try for roles opposite hers so they could exchange intimate glances on stage. "He was a virgin," Mona had confided to Annie. "Can you believe it? I thought virgins didn't *exist* anymore. I had to initiate him. Me, the teacher!"

"I take it he caught on."

"Clyde's sexuality is"—Mona held forth her hands as though they cupped water—"his whole body. The only thing he doesn't know from instinct is how to hold back, the way all those other men do."

Early in the semester Annie had given Mona a key to her apartment, so the lovers wouldn't have to hold back on account of Mona's housemates. They came by once or twice a week while Annie was at the theater, and they always left flowers or wine to let her know they appreciated the gesture. Around the campus Mona and Clyde sauntered hand in hand, dressed in sweatshirts and jeans, and Mona rarely talked about losing weight anymore. Her body was softened by a Grecian layer of supple flesh which always looked warm and which graced even her dodges and feints on the tennis court.

"That's your game, and I've got to go," Mona said. "You're playing awfully well today."

"Thanks. I feel good."

"I hope so. Remember, I've been there."

It's not the same place, Annie wanted to say—but how did she know it wasn't? Though she had won it, the tennis match had twisted her afternoon with Philip. "I'm not sure I know what I'm doing," she said as they walked up the hill from the courts.

"But you've got to do it, don't you?" Mona's face took on an old and wise look, camouflaging the anger. "You've got to go to him. You can't help yourself, and nobody else can stop you."

◇　　◇　　◇　　◇　　◇　　◇　　◇　　◇　　◇

Back at her apartment Annie showered. She stood with her back to the spray, letting the hot water hammer her shoulders and neck until she could feel the little knots of muscle letting go. She threw the tennis clothes into a pillowcase tacked onto the bathroom door and dressed in a long cotton skirt. The apartment was stifling, dark as usual, shaded after ten o'clock by the oak tree. The building was one of a small group of gray stucco garages with rooms above, owned by the college and inhabited by students who seemed to lock themselves in and disappear. All the buildings were condemned, and none was big enough to house a party, so those who rented them were mostly odd, reclusive types who left clay sculptures standing in the yard or kept pet snakes. Annie rented out the garage below her place to a botany major named Christopher who had taken a leave this term, leaving her with his ficus and dracaena.

She opened a window and put the kettle on to heat. Dishes were piled in the sink. Picking one out, she rinsed it and poured a bowl of cereal. She took poor care of the apartment—Mona was always telling her so. She let dust collect on the furniture, and she never made the bed. Drawers in the maple desk and dresser hung open. She had started to paint the main room once, but after two walls she ran out of paint, so the other two remained, the same ivory color but dingier, like the unbleached dress in an ad.

Then, tacked around the room like newspaper clippings, hung her design sketches. Their thick deckled paper, their unerring India-ink outlines, the dots and splashes of bright acrylic seemed intrusive, almost arrogant here in this cubbyhole of a room. Sample fabrics were stapled at the sides, and a straight line ran from the cloth to its place in the sketch. Somehow the hangings had managed to remain clean, and in the dull light the paper shone as if phosphorescent. Philip had noticed them. She wondered what he had thought—that they were trivial, probably.

With her coffee and cereal, Annie sat at the small table by the kitchen window, where the sun still shone in. She had a class on German mysticism with Jack Wheelbright in five minutes, but she couldn't bring herself to go, especially when it meant seeing Jack. Would Philip have talked to him, about her? No, of course not.

Annie had never known what to do about Jack Wheelbright. He was a tall and angular man, with a broad, flat face stamped by intelligence and gunshot-gray eyes that flashed dramatically when he wanted his students to come to life or when he wanted Annie Redfield to notice him. Like other inspired teachers he was a manic depressive, as Annie had realized soon after the initial flattery of his attention wore off. Now she teased him and played the innocent with him, and she endured his long, maudlin soliloquies, but she relied on him too. She had depended on his solicitude in a cowardly and selfish way that she didn't like in herself, and when he took her out to drink and talk, she had always let him think there was a great mystery behind her silences. She needed him to think that, and to give her his flimsy, eager sympathy. But that would change, henceforth—everything would change.

From the window she could see across the street and past the parking lot to the theater, on this side a modern geometric structure, white cement with exposed girders. Around the corner, just out of sight, was the old part of the building, with the fire escape that led to the costume studio. The room had been built as a kind of afterthought over the new theater, and when she was working Annie could hear the sounds of rehearsal echoing through the catwalk before they thudded into the concrete ceiling. The windows along the slanting south roof opened outward, like those in an artist's loft. The whole structure had just been completed the year before Annie came to Newhall, and the first time she had seen the room there were no closets or wardrobes or even shelves in it—it was just a concrete box, cold and dusty. But the sun through the windows had looked promising, and without thinking she had already claimed the space for her own.

Annie had always wanted to design for the theater. As a child she had filled sketchbooks with a Nutcracker that grew more and more glorious until he outshone even the Prince, and while the other students in her drawing classes were concentrating on naked breasts and legs, she was inventing ways to disguise them. It was something she could do well, as it turned out, and so she had left the art studio and gone straight home from school to seek her trade. For her fourteenth birthday she got an easel, a set of acrylics, and her India-ink pen; for her fifteenth, a commercial sewing machine and exclusive rights to the basement. When no boys asked her out on the weekends, and they often didn't, she could descend to her world of drawings and textiles and breathe life into them. The boys didn't ask because she was too tall and because she would hardly speak to them. She didn't speak because she didn't know what to say. It was not until she was preparing to leave Grosse Pointe that a friend's brother, a sculpture student at Columbia, came home for the summer and dug Annie out of the basement. "You're the one," he had told her, dressed in his khakis and turtleneck, rubbing his rich beard against her cheek. "You're going to be chosen. Again and again. Christ, just look at that mouth of yours." And he had molded her lips with his own.

When she got to Newhall the theater director had said they didn't have funds for a wardrobe mistress, though they had applied for a part-time position. But no, he hadn't thought of hiring a student. When the money came through he would need a professional; after all, the department at Newhall was quite well known.

Then he had seen her credits. By that time, working out of the lonely basement, she had won the Young Designer's Prize for a commedia dell'arte version of *Fantasio,* a scholarship to Ashland, a commission from the Ann Arbor ballet. He thought maybe a student would work out after all; would she consider four hundred a month plus three units of credit? Then they could hire her an assistant. They would scrounge the funds somewhere.

There had been a new assistant to Annie every year. Now it was Ellen Cox, a bright, overweight sophomore who was almost ready to give up dreams of acting. But the studio wasn't the same when Ellen was there, or when the other students getting their unit of credit were there, running up hems and talking about movie actors and asking Annie questions as if she were the teacher. She had made up a schedule so she worked with them only once a week, when she handed out assignments and checked seams and arranged for Ellen to run the workshop with them on Wednesday night. She tried to imitate the gently tough designer from New York who had run the shop at Ashland to perfection, with the air of one who didn't know how all this had come about but here she was with the answers. The rest of the week, Annie could slip up the fire escape at odd times and have the room all to herself. Coming from the apartment, she felt like a mole blinking in the bright sun. She would straighten and rearrange the shelves, after three years still smelling of fresh plywood; she would clear scraps out of the corners; she would prop up the windows and let the breeze shake out the hanging dresses. She knew that, right now, piled neatly on the cutting table lay the pieces for Roxanne's dress in *Cyrano,* and she could as much as feel the watery satin sliding through her hands.

She put the dishes back in the sink and combed her damp hair, then headed down the steps and across the street. This would be a good time to work and a good time, while she worked, to absorb Philip, the fact of Philip and what was happening to her.

"Annie!"

She stopped on the bottom step of the fire escape. Jack Wheelbright appeared from around the corner of the building. "I thought you had a class," she said.

"I thought you did too. The same class, if I recall rightly."

"I overslept. I didn't want to come in late and interrupt."

"I see. Well, I let the class go early."

"Why?"

"*You* weren't there. What else could I do?" Jack's eyes twinkled in his practiced way. "You'll have lunch with me, anyway. To make up the lecture you missed."

"I can't—I've got to finish a costume."

"Tomorrow, then."

"Tomorrow I have a noon class."

"Thursday?"

"No, I—no, not Thursday. Thursday afternoon's an awfully busy one for me." Annie felt herself grow suddenly warm. Philip was coming by on Thursday to see her without her clothes. My face gives it away, she thought.

"Well, are you going to make me tick off all the days of the week, or will you say when?"

"Friday. Friday'll be fine."

"Okay. Be in my office at twelve. I do want to talk with you. We'll go out for Mexican food."

Emily had a runny nose, and Joan just thought it was sniffles, but Philip had been watching for a while and he suspected his daughter was allergic. He took her to the clinic on Wednesday afternoon, and they diagnosed her as reactive to cats, dogs, trees, weeds, and house dust. Emily was good all through the testing, silent tears just starting from her eyes when they pricked her arm the fourth or fifth time, while Didi at that age would have bawled and jerked out of the doctor's reach. On the way home Emily was excited; her face still pale from noiseless crying, she repeated, "Cats, dogs, trees, weeds, house dust!" like a jingle as she bounced on the front seat.

When Joan got home and learned the diagnosis, she kissed each of Emily's scars from the testing, saying, "There's the cat. Meow. There's the dust," until Emily couldn't stand up from giggling.

"It's a shame, though," Joan said after dinner. "Means I can't take her into the field with me anymore. The pollen would drive her nuts."

"Hadn't you noticed it driving her nuts before?"

"Not really. A few sniffles. What'll she do, get shots?"

It irritated Philip that Joan never noticed things. He had found it charming twenty-two years ago, but by now he thought she should be more aware. She had a job where she spotted rare birds from miles away, where she had to be attuned to the slightest signs, but she couldn't remember what Didi had said on the phone or notice the corrosion under the kitchen sink.

"They want us to try keeping the house clean and the cat out of her room. Maybe she'll grow out of it, but for now we can keep the level of allergens down and see about shots later."

"Oh, all right. Should we get her a foam pillow?"

"No. That's for mold. She doesn't react to mold."

"Don't get snappy. We're not all medical experts."

"Just anticipating the hassle," Philip said. Joan turned back to the map she had tacked on the kitchen wall, and he went to the door to the living room, where Emily was picking out an unmelodic tune on her small electric piano. Already her body was lengthening, the neck and torso slimmed down; the straight blond hair she had inherited from Joan had lost its baby fineness and taken on a little-girl shimmer. She was in first grade now, gone the whole day from home, and while her absence made his own schedule much easier, he missed watching her grow.

Joan hadn't wanted a second child, and when she became pregnant she had wanted to terminate it. Philip had persuaded her with two promises: that he would do the lion's share of parenting and that he would have a vasectomy. He had kept his part of the arrangement, but it made him "snappy," as Joan put it, to know he would have to cover Emily's mattress in plastic, train the cat to stay out, worry that the allergies might develop into asthma. Joan would only need to forgo an occasional outing in the bird sanctuary. It was a peculiar bargain they had struck, and pulled him in conflicting directions.

"Didi called," Joan said.

"What for?" He kept his eyes on Emily, who had looked up to get his approval and then gone on playing.

"To wish me happy birthday."

"Your birthday's tomorrow."

"She has an exam tomorrow—she thought it might make her forget. She also said she'd be home the sixteenth for Christmas."

"Christ, they let them go early, up there."

"She also asked," said Joan, coming up beside him, "if we'd made any more plans."

"Plans?"

"About your leave. Next year." She stood next to him in the narrow doorway, and he rested his arm around her. She fit neatly under his shoulder, her face even with his chest. Tomorrow she would be forty-four. Tomorrow, he thought calmly as they both listened to Emily's one-handed, stumbling version of "Toyland," he would be making love with a woman half Joan's age. The curves that life threw you. He had not thought once, since he entered Annie's apartment the day before, about his leave.

"We still have to see if we can spring *you,* don't we?" he asked.

"Depends if the grant goes through."

Joan was a research associate for the Anacapa Bird Observatory, which had originally concerned itself with shore birds. But four years ago, with the rapidly dwindling population of the California condor demanding attention, the U.S. Fish and Wildlife Service had created the Condor Recovery Team, headquartered at the Anacapa Observatory, to track the birds and evaluate their nesting patterns with an eye toward eventually capturing one to mate at the San Diego Zoo with Topa, the only condor in captivity. For three years now, the federal grant had enabled the team to do fieldwork but hadn't allowed for trapping a bird which fell under the Endangered Species Act. Until the sex of Topa could be determined, the government had decreed that the mating scheme would be a mere gamble, not worth the cost or the risk of losing a single one of the sensitive birds.

A recent blood study, however, had shown Topa to be a female, and the observatory had petitioned for permission and funds to capture a male bird. Joan spent her days in the mountains, scanning the air for the huge buzzards, watching them nest, and looking in vain for eggs or young birds—anticipating the go-ahead.

"If you get the money," Philip said, "I guess you'll have to stay here."

"Well, I won't find a mate for Topa in England, but I could take a few months off. Are you so set on going next year?"

"I don't know." He met her pale eyes and noticed the faint mauve-tinted rings that had begun to encircle them. He was anticipating the morrow; next year was worlds away, "We could put it on hold." Put everything on hold. Suspend oneself in the risk at hand. Until the connection snaps. He touched his wife's forehead with the back of a finger.

"No," said Joan. "We'll go."

At that moment Emily finished her piece. They turned to her and clapped.

◇   ◇   ◇   ◇   ◇   ◇   ◇   ◇   ◇

The restaurant was dark and smelled of salt and chili paste. Jack was on his second beer; he had finished the basket of tortilla chips. Smoking a cigarette, Annie listened to the mariachi players and watched them in their sequined jackets, wandering like fireflies around the room.

"So how've you been?" Jack asked. His voice seemed to come from far away. His wooden body bent forward from the waist, his prominent forehead and wide-set eyes staring out like the features of a handsomely dressed-up skull. Annie let out a cloud of smoke. Her mind was on Philip.

"Fine. I've been fine."

"You look different."

"Got my hair cut."

"How's Philip?"

Annie steadied her eyes on him. She thought how Philip trusted her—he'd known she would be good at this. "He's fine, I guess. Was there something wrong with him?"

"No, it's just that I see so little of him these days. To tell the truth, I think he's been avoiding me."

"Nonsense. His students see little of him too—he must be a busy guy."

"I wanted to talk to him about Ruth. He knows her, and he's my closest associate among the faculty here. In spite of the difference in age, you see, we have been close. Do you know how old he is?"

"In his forties, I guess."

"Forty-five. And I'm thirty-three." Hinting broadly, he twinkled his eyes.

"At your ages I shouldn't think that would be any barrier to friendship," Annie said.

"No. No, it's not."

The waitress took their orders and refilled the basket of chips. Jack had begun to tear at his napkin and to pile the shreds neatly in the ashtray, where the embers from Annie's cigarette singed the paper. "What about Ruth?" Annie asked.

"Well, it's gotten pretty heavy between us, and now I'm afraid she might go back to Edgar."

"Who's Edgar?"

"Her husband. You should know him. He teaches in the art department—Edgar Baumann. He's also into Hinduism. He's shaved his head."

"Don't know him."

"Anyway, he doesn't mind our relationship, but he doesn't want a divorce. See, it was all his idea in the first place—he decided last year that he should be celibate, but he didn't want to impose abstinence on Ruth. So he tried for months to get me to sleep with her instead. He thought it should be a white man. Do you mind my telling you all this?"

"No, not at all. It's fascinating."

"I didn't want to be part of their plan for a long while. Not that I didn't want her, but I worried about Edgar's real feelings. Then one day she came over and it just happened—you know how things happen. Which made *everybody* happy. But then her emotions got involved, and mine got heavily involved, and Edgar hadn't expected that. . . ."

Philip, Annie thought. Philip. By repeating his name to herself, like a magic word, she could bring the touch and the smell of him to her senses, and the restaurant and Jack and his soap opera disappeared like so much unnecessary scenery.

She had waited for him in the room, at first, yesterday; then she had grown fidgety and done some hand wash. When she had finished, she took the damp clothes outside and hung them on the line to dry. He would see that as sensual, she knew, the dripping clothes and the water running down her bare arms into her rolled-up sleeves. He had found her there, in the broad daylight, and he had come with her up the steps as if he were just one person visiting another. She had felt as he undressed her that she had never wanted anyone ever before. She had felt herself a lake filling with water, reaching the edge, with relief spilling over the dam.

"Do you think I am a jealous man?" Jack asked, pulling her attention back.

"Mm? Yes, I should think you would be. Not envious. Possessive."

He drew in his chin, hurt. "I never thought I was, but when Ruth talks about continuing to live with him, I can't think straight. I'm afraid she tells him what we do, all the ways we make love. We do some pretty weird things, you know."

Jack had finished his enchilada and was picking at his beans, moving them around the plate with his fork. His face allowed no humor or relief. He wanted her to ask about the weird things. "I've got to go," Annie said. "I'm meeting an acting workshop. They need costumes."

"Is that a lie?"

"Of course not. We've been here two hours, Jack. Here, let's split the bill."

"Not on your life. My treat. Someone's been telling you I'm a tightwad."

"You think you'll be able to stay with Ruth, on her terms?" Annie asked as they drove back.

"She's saving me, saving my soul. I have to."

"Good, then."

"Yes, it is, and I'm happy. Really I am. But you know, if you had given one sign—this would never have come about."

Jack's voice played a light and suggestive tune, but his eyes as he looked at Annie were greedy, like an insect's. She sighed gladly when he let her out.

Thanksgiving was heaven. That Friday, Joan took Emily to a carnival on the grounds of the Child's Garden Zoo forty miles away in Santa Barbara; they would not return until after dinner.

Philip picked Annie up at the corner near her apartment shortly before noon, and they drove the ten miles up Topatopa Mountain to the east side of the range and the two-thousand-acre condor refuge where Joan did her fieldwork. Annie's ears popped as they climbed higher, and she caught a glimpse of the Pacific, an hour to the west of Newhall. The road up Topatopa turned to dirt three miles from the entrance to the refuge, and the wind blew the dust they had raised back onto the car. When they got out, Annie took a deep breath of the light, dry air and had to take a step to keep her balance. "My God, I'm giddy already," she said.

"That's Reyes Peak, to the west," said Philip. "On the other side there's a large valley, then the Sierra Madre." The mountains shone stark and blue in the sun; there was no lush vegetation anywhere. Behind them, the pines rustled like paper shuffling, and the ferns on the roadside had let splay their crinkled brown leaves. By the sign for the refuge was a square placard with slots for interchangeable words, reading "Fire Danger Today: *Very High.*"

"I hope the rains come soon," Annie said. "This place is parched."

"A month or so," said Philip.

Cars were not allowed in the refuge. Philip had parked by the fence and they walked in, Annie carrying a basket, following a fire road by a dry creekbed. "You can't really see any of the birds from here," Philip explained. "They've left a buffer zone at least a couple of miles around the territory the condors actually inhabit, so that noise doesn't frighten them. But there don't seem to be many birds of any sort out today."

"Too hot for them."

"Actually, that's true—it is the wrong time of day."

"Morning would be better?"

"Yes—though I'd hoped to at least spot some Stellar's jays, up this high. Look there!"

Annie shaded her eyes. "What is it?"

"Red-tailed hawk, I'm pretty certain."

"Surely you can't see the red tail from here."

"No, but there are other characteristics. I should have brought field glasses. Watch how it circles."

The hawk spiraled slowly above them, then dived without warning into the chapparal. "A mouse, probably," Philip said, "or a rabbit. That's about the biggest prey left."

They crossed the streambed. Pine and eucalyptus grew on the other side, and there was more growth in the trees' shade. Opening the basket, Annie unfolded her striped Mexican blanket and spread it over a patch of ground, hidden from the fire road. "Have you ever seen a condor?" she asked.

"No. I get all my information from Joan."

Annie leaned back against the needles which softened the ground. "Joan," she said. "I can't make her exist, for me. I try to get a clear picture of her, I try to imagine that part of your life, but nothing comes through."

"Here's where she works. Does that help?"

"How did she get involved with condors?"

He shrugged. "A penchant for lost causes, I guess."

"Is that why you brought me here—to show me about her?"

"No."

"Why, then?"

"I just thought it was a nice spot. You shouldn't worry about Joan, Annie. She has nothing to do with you."

Annie smiled. She recalled Mona's recitations of the sins of Bruce, one of which had been to claim that his wife was in a separate emotional realm. Just yesterday, in the drugstore, Annie had spotted Joan Decker—had recognized her for the first time because she had been with Philip's daughter Emily buying allergy medicine. She had looked old to be Emily's mother, with her wispy blond-gray hair, her short, trim figure and full breasts. She wore large sunglasses which masked her face, though underneath Annie could spot a nervous eye-blinking tic and a curious pulling on the mouth. Annie had tried to gauge the size of the breasts and how they had looked two decades ago. "Does she understand you?" she asked Philip now.

"Yes. I think she does."

Annie reached into the basket. She would not make Joan her battle. "I brought everything elegant I could find in Newhall," she said. "Pâté, artichoke hearts, fresh bread, champagne. No caviar."

Philip uncorked the champagne. "California Extra Dry," he read, and laughed. "Perfect."

"Can we make love here?"

"No. Too risky."

"Nobody would see us."

"I know." Philip poured the amber liquid into two plastic glasses, then sat holding them both, looking away from Annie. "That's not quite true, what I said about why I brought you here," he said. "I am trying to express something. But not to you."

"Maybe to Joan. This is her territory."

"But she's not here. Maybe to myself. I think I just wanted to see how it would feel, seeing you here."

"How does it feel?"

"I don't know. Dangerous. Let's eat and go back to your place."

"Not till I've had some sun."

"Oh, there's plenty of time for that," he said, handing her the glass of champagne.

After the holiday weekend it was suddenly December. The month passed quickly, marked off not by the steady layering of snow and grip of cold Annie had known in Michigan, but by the time Philip could steal to be with her. Like a tulip sprung from its bulb for a passing season, their circumscribed meetings quickly took on a full-blossomed, unchanging form. Tuesday and Thursday afternoons, after 1:15 class, before Emily came home from school and Annie's studio hours began, Philip came over and they went to bed.

Making love was terrific. That was the word Philip used, and it was the right word. Sometimes they undressed each other slowly, beginning with shoes and fastenings, but mostly Annie had little on—she planned for him and would shower and wait in her kimono. As he sat on her bed she knelt behind him and unbuttoned his shirt. By the time he was naked they were both swollen from wanting, and Annie could feel the pulse of her heart as if it beat between her legs. He always touched her breasts first, experimentally, then he moved down to kiss her belly and mount of Venus. Annie succumbed to his skill, and as he entered and moved in her, she reached her hands over his wide back and she came, always. She didn't tell him she had never come before.

Philip got in his application for a fall leave by the middle of December. He couldn't have written a more ideal prospectus for the symposium in England. They were going to look at the mind-body question from every angle—identity, memory, hormone theory, split-brain experiments; even imagination, the phenomenon Annie was trying to pin down in her thesis. Rawlins, the Oxford don organizing it all, wrote to ask if Philip would convene a series of papers that could be published as the first collection on the philosophy of biology. When Didi came home on the sixteenth—heavier, he noticed, with her hair cut in a longish shag that made her look uncared for—he began his arguments to make her come along.

"Take a semester at Oxford," he said. "Learn what it's like to have to really *think*."

"We think at Berkeley." She smiled archly at him.

"You don't have to live with us. You could stay in university housing."

"Daddy, I don't know where I'll be a year from now," Didi pleaded, laughing at him. "I don't even know if I'll want to be in *school*."

There was a guy in her life, she told him that night. Eugene, a business major. She showed Philip his picture. "Don't worry, I've got birth control," she said proudly. He hadn't expected her *not* to have birth control. But what he also hadn't expected was for the guy to look so limp, so easily manhandled by his daughter. He wanted more for her, just as he had wanted more for himself. "I'm not that crazy about him," Didi said when she saw the look on Phililp's face. "It's just somebody to hang out with."

He could not in his turn show her a picture of Annie Redfield, a slender, long-waisted woman two years older than Didi, dressed in knickers and boots or a thick embroidered skirt. As the holidays approached and he spent more time with his daughters, he doubted the wisdom of beginning this affair in the first place. He had never known anyone with Annie's sense of gravity and lightness in everything about the mind and the body. His women had been hardheaded, smart, explainable. He was out of his element with Annie, true though it was that they spoke the same language. "We'll always be hiding," she had said that week, and Philip knew that for a love affair to last it needed the open air. Even for Annie, as she pinched back her smile and averted her eyes from him on campus, the early thrill of the embrace in a dark corner had been short-lived and would grow cancerous. But the step couldn't be reversed, so soon; the moments of having her had not begun to outstrip the weeks of wanting her.

Then Annie left, abruptly and without farewell, it seemed, to be with her parents in Michigan until classes resumed. He had not thought of her as having family. People like Joan and himself had families, responsibilities they had spawned and woven into the tight fabric of their lives. People like Annie floated free. But suddenly she was gone to people he did not know and rarely heard about, and when she was telling them stories of her life, he would not be included. The Tuesday afternoon after she was gone he could do nothing right—he forgot to pick Emily up at school until she called in tears, he broke off the top of the Christmas tree squeezing it into the living room. Distracted, he called Urban Whittaker to ask if he wanted to drive to Las Vegas and do a little gambling over the weekend.

"Are you crazy, man?" said Urban. "It's the week before fucking Christmas! Harriet's brother and his kids are here, and I'm supposed to chauffeur them all into L.A. for the *Nutcracker*. Vegas doesn't *exist*, this time of year."

"It exists. Luck rides high at the end of the year."

"You," said Urban, his voice gravelly on the phone, "are itchy. You want my advice?"

"No."

"Repot your bonsai. Fuck Joan. Read Epictetus."

"Epictetus was a zombie," Philip said, though he didn't think so, and hung up.

The bonsai occupied most of the screen porch off the kitchen. There were a dozen of them, dwarfed trees over fifty years old and no more than two feet high, and they were Philip's one private hobby. It was a careful process, wiring the small trunks and branches to force a certain shape, amputating one or two large limbs early on, clipping back tendrils and roots to stunt the trees' constant effort to grow. Their branches were etchings in the air, flocked with perfect leaves, and two of them, the Chinese wisteria and cotoneaster, bloomed for three weeks in April.

"I think it's cruel, and I'll always think it's cruel, and I'll never forgive you for it," Didi said, appearing at the screened door.

"Plants do not have minds. You can't be cruel to them."

"That's what they used to say about Chinese women as they bound their feet."

"Plants are controlled everywhere. Think of lawns and hedges."

"It doesn't seem as . . . *deliberate,* somehow," Didi said, wincing as her father pruned a top branch. "Ooh, it hurts to watch."

But she stood and watched nonetheless as he tended the trees. He knew what Didi was saying, though it made no logical sense. It matched what she used to say about fishing. The truth was that he enjoyed the severity of the discipline. Bonsai were not bonsai if every trace of uncontrolled growth were not erased vigilantly, and a bonsai allowed to grow beyond the limits of its beauty became not a normal tree but a freak, bent and twisted into itself, bound for an early death. Each careful cut, each twist of the wire hurt not the plant but himself, and he knew the ascetic's thrill at the pain. Urban had been right: the urge to see Annie was put to sleep in a corner of his mind, he had taken charge of the day.

"Remember how you used to take me out to the desert?" Didi said.

"You mean like last summer?"

"No, I mean like in the spring, when you and I used to go. To see the wildflowers, you know, and the cactus when it bloomed."

"Ah. You mean when we'd go *gliding*."

"Yeah. You knew the names of everything—you could even identify them from the air. I can't remember a single one."

"Oh, come on. Wild pieplant."

"Strawberry cactus."

"Turban cactus."

"Um . . . See, I can't do any more. All those names and patterns and characteristics. When they bloom, how the fruit tastes, acid or sweet. They stick in my head, but they're mixed up."

"We'll have to go again soon, I can see that."

"I was wondering." Didi straddled a stool and brushed dead leaves from the counter. "If I dropped out of school in the spring, we could take a trip out there."

"If you came home over spring break, we could take the same trip." Philip spread a thin layer of mulch around the base of the wisteria. "Do you want to drop out of school?"

"I don't know. I just keep thinking about . . . spending time with you. When I was younger. I learned so much more."

Philip peered at his daughter, his favorite in the family. He remembered those days clearly, when they had taken the road that snaked around Cobblestone Mountain to the place where they rented a glider. Like a bird—he used to point at a hawk, to demonstrate—the plane would rise with the warm air flow and descend in the cold spots. He'd explained to Didi how there was nothing to fear as the plane sank, but she had never been afraid. "Got one!" she would announce in the air, her high voice whipped away by the wind, and Philip would take the draft, tilt the plane sharply upward, and begin to circle. Didi had always gotten nauseated as the plane coiled through the thin air, and she would shut her eyes until he told her they were on top of it and she could look down onto the bald mountaintop and the patch-work glory of the desert below.

She was the only one he had taken to the desert. He would take her again, if she visited in the spring. But he didn't want Didi living here, in the same town with Annie. Didi had found out about Linda; now she was older and smarter. And no one needed to be hurt; he had found that by carrying these things off well, no one was even touched. *But why don't you tell me?* her eyes still asked.

"Why don't you finish the year," he said, measuring three-quarters of a cup of water and giving it to the wisteria, "and then take time in England?"

"I want to come home, Daddy." She went to the screen door and crossed her arms, looking over the dry brown grass of their backyard. "I can't think straight at Berkeley. Everyone there's on some path or other—"

"Even Eugene?"

"*Especially* Eugene. And you always told me not to get too set about my future."

"I said that?"

"You did. On the desert. I remember," she spoke rapidly, "it was after we'd been gliding, we'd gone for drinks at the Cattle-man. You remember how we always stopped at the Cattleman? And you told me you didn't really like what you'd grown up to be. That sometime you'd change."

"I'd change," he repeated.

"And I said I wouldn't care. Well, I want to change too."

"You're young, Didi! You're always changing."

"No, I mean change *inside*. I have to come home to do it. I have to have you there."

Abruptly she went out the screen door, letting it slam behind her. He watched her stride across the driveway onto the path that cut through to the next street. As he let her go, he surprised himself by whispering aloud, "Just give me a little time. Please." He had to outrun them, his family and his work. Didi wanted him to play the father-teacher; the others wanted other roles. Only Annie wanted him whole, as he was, without expectations.

Philip laid down his trowel. Urban's bonsai idea hadn't worked after all. Joan was up at the mountain, so he couldn't make love to her. He went inside to wash his hands and then pulled a volume of Epictetus off his shelf, but when he sat down, instead of reading it, he flipped through his desk calendar. Twelve days until she'd be back. He'd just have to start counting.

It was in January that Mona began to drift away, but in the short days and desert-cold nights Annie felt nothing more than time slipping between her fingers. After classes she waited for Philip, pacing the room while sketches lay half finished and books lay unopened on her desk. Once he had left she could catch up. He would set his watch on her nightstand so he wouldn't stay too long. Twice he had fallen asleep, and Annie, wanting to break the watch instead, had had to shake him and send him home.

There was the other time schedule, too—-the eight months that had shortened to seven, then six. A phone call to say he couldn't come lopped off another day. Against her passion Annie found herself establishing emotional allowances, determined to break the spell in June. To love well and leave, she thought—that was what Mona had not been able to do.

But she didn't see much of Mona anymore. It was too chilly in the early morning for tennis, and they hadn't picked another time of day to play. Clyde had moved in with Mona, in the house she shared with four other women in the theater, and Annie saw them all often strolling together across the campus, Clyde like a happy sheepdog in a group of sleek dachshunds and Airedales. Once over Christmas Mona had called from Philadelphia, the line crackling, to say she was bored and Bruce of all people had sent her a necklace for a present. They hadn't spoken of Philip, and Annie knew now that was why Mona had called, because Michigan and Philadelphia were neutral ground. For herself, she had passed the time with her brother Gerald and his wife and new baby, and baby-sitting her twin siblings, George and Lisa. She had filled her suitcase with the dusty library books Philip had told her to read, and she had pored over them until she was dizzy. After making notes and writing out ideas, she had thrown the pages away. Christmas dinner had been at her father's house, where the shrill new Mrs. Redfield had complained about the price of meat while Annie's father showed postcards of all the places he'd been that year, from New York to Argentina.

It had been comforting to be accepted and forgotten. But Annie's mother had noticed something. Mrs. Redfield had grown up deep in the South, in a forgotten part of the country where things relied more on ritual but curiously less on morality. She knew how to make a gesture. "Annie dear," she had said the last morning—it was she who had christened Annie, after her own mother, with the diminutive of the name—"you usually have such a good color when you come home. Have you been ill?"

Annie had put aside the sketch she was drawing. "No, just inside a lot, working on costumes and my thesis."

"You aren't worried about some boy, are you?"

"No, Mom." Annie had thought she should invent a nice boyfriend for her, all bright eyes and straight teeth, but she couldn't.

"Aren't you seeing anyone at all?"

"Not really. Well, yes. Sort of. Different people, in the theater—you know."

"Well." Her mother had patted Annie's shoulder and picked up the sketches that lay scattered on the floor. "You don't have to tell me, but if you ever do, I'll try not to play the old lady. I'd like to know, sometime."

"They'd all like to know," Annie said to Philip late in January, over lunch. Lunch was their consolation for hiding and waiting, their escape from Annie's dark room, her chance to laugh away any guilt over Mona. With a couple of professors (often Jack) or students tagging along after class, a pitcher of beer, and talk of syllogisms or Cartesian myth or the school administration, lunch was practically a ritual. But to Annie even the tag-alongs seemed hawklike, hungry for the meat of gossip.

"Sure, they'd like to know," Philip said. "They smell out a

mystery. They want to be struck by the same—what would you call it—lightning?"

When, like today, she could get Philip away from the others, they went to Charlie's, a place two miles from campus and generally unknown. They got clam chowder and beer for a dollar and took a booth in a corner, and sometimes they still had debates. Annie liked that. The rhythm of the argument was not unlike sex—they never railed against one another but thrust and parried, the tension building, then giving way. Annie leaned forward, earnest and maddeningly articulate; Philip let his cigarette burn between his fingers while he drew graphs and syllogisms to show her the higher nonsense of her ideas. Now he was waving her thesis, the part she'd finished over Christmas, at her.

"Christ, don't bring metaphor in," he said. " 'The slings and arrows of outrageous fortune.' It's confusing and meaningless and only weakens your already weak case."

"How weakens? Shakespeare knew what he was saying and said it the most efficient way he could."

"What slings? Where are the arrows?"

"In fortune. The objective correlative. They're not literary slings, they're *real* slings. Look." She took the pencil with which he had been drawing arrows and writing "Fortune?" and held it up. "What color is this pencil?"

"Yellow."

"Find me another way to say that."

"That's got nothing to do with it. Given sufficient time and paper I could set down, in graphic objective language, what Shakespeare meant by his figure of speech. The pencil is different."

"Not at all. You could tell me what chemicals combined to make this dye, how light acting on the pigment affects its appearance to the beholder, how certain shades of light affect said appearance in predeterminable ways. You still won't have told me the pencil is yellow." She rolled it between her fingers, the color reflected in the varnish of the table.

"Actually, that's a thought. Maybe I could, given that you

understood my terminology and the logical outcome of my calculations."

"But it's certainly not the most effective way to communicate the sensory quality, the yellowness of the pencil."

"But it might be the clearest. It undoubtedly is, when you compare it to a combination of arrows, which are actual, and fortune, which is theoretical."

"Well, then, supposing Shakespeare to be a playwright of average intelligence, why'd he do it?"

"For the rhyme scheme."

Annie snorted.

"Okay, then, for the beauty, the lift it gives the imagination."

"That reduces all art—metaphor is the *core* of art, you realize—to a piece of fluff."

"That doesn't necessarily follow."

Philip had finished his beer and was signaling for another. Annie was pleasantly fuming, aiming the pencil, like an arrow, at his chest. Like some alien being, the waitress at Charlie's stepped inside their circle to deliver the beer and empty the ashtray; she had bright red hair, Annie noticed, and cracked her gum.

Philip was interested in the argument or in using his mind or in her—maybe some of each. They ordered many beers. We speak to each other, Annie thought sometime in January, through screens—through the intellectual battles, through talk of Jack or others we know, through touch and sex. But we never really speak to each other.

She memorized his looks. The thin hair was gray, very gray. The face was large and rough, but she had seen a picture of him when he had first arrived at Newhall, and he had looked like Marlon Brando. The eyes were bluer than hers—steel blue—and the eyebrows slanted up toward the middle, giving him a puzzled expression. He was tall, broad at the shoulders, with a back so set in muscle it was difficult for her to massage. Beer was affecting his belly. He walked with quick, long strides, like one hurrying to be on time. She loved to watch him walk. She loved to watch him pace back and forth before the lectern, dressed in blue, stopping to rest a leg on a chair and point sideways at a student with a question. She loved to watch him smoke, which he did expertly and too much. She didn't like to see him take out his half-glasses or hear him cough, but she loved to stroke his short hands and feel him settle into her worn armchair while she curled at his feet.

"You know I'm teaching a course at UCLA this term," Philip said. It was the second week of February, and he had called Annie into his office before class.

"Sure. I drove in with you last week, for the afternoon."

"Well, I won't be driving back after the next class." A slow grin came over his face, and Annie mirrored it, not knowing why. "I have to give a lecture on the philosophy of biology to a group of doctors Friday morning. The speech is set for eight o'clock, and it's a two-hour drive."

"So you're spending the night?"

"Joan and I decided it would be more practical than heading home in rush-hour traffic and then driving back in before dawn."

"And I take it you'd like company."

"Well, that's what I had in mind, yes."

At first it seemed unbelievable—a whole night, dusk to dawn. Then almost immediately it was inevitable. Of course they would spend the night together; it had to happen sometime. Instead of drinking coffee and sitting cross-legged on her bed in the morning light, it would be a cheap motel by the beach, that was all.

As she left class, Annie realized she was frightened. Her knees shook as she descended the broad stone steps of the building. She wanted to call Mona, and she even walked past the Counseling Center, a purposefully nonthreatening little brick house on the edge of campus which threatened her with neat diagnoses of her love affair each time she passed by. "And have you never gotten along with your father?" they would have asked. "How satisfied are you with younger men, sexually speaking?" She peeked in the door that afternoon, to see if there was anyone there who looked as if they knew more than she did and could be kind, but she saw only faces which looked like other faces, and a secretary.

She wanted to ask somebody what the odds were, on being able to go back, after a whole night together, to the short and furtive meetings and the end. She couldn't help thinking it was dangerous, accustomed to hiding away as they were, to go out into the light even once, pretending they could retreat again.

Thursday morning she closeted herself away as if packing were some kind of ceremony. She washed her face, picked at it, washed it again, soaked it with astringent. It had broken out, a condition she minded mostly because of its association with adolescence, when strangely enough her skin had been fair and unflawed. Just under her cheekbones, high and delicate, she rubbed spots of blushing gel, spreading it to her chin to offset the paleness brought on by nerves. Her hair was cut in the only style she had found to accommodate its curly fineness, and she brushed it until it crackled and stood out from her head. The day would be soft and cool; she dug through her closet and rejected most of the mufti she had gathered for her wardrobe, silks and patched leathers and antique rayon dresses. Finally she pulled out a pair of brown velour pants and a challis blouse, and when she had dressed she felt suddenly easier. Her small overnight bag was nearly empty—a change of clothes, a sweater, a toothbrush. Nightie? she could hear her mother saying. No, of course not a nightie. Maybe a robe. Perfume in her purse. When she had closed the case, she sat on the bed and lit a cigarette. She puffed, tried to inhale, coughed, reached for a glass of water, and noticed her hand was shaking.

Control, she told herself. These things had started happening to her lately: nervous perspiration, shaky hands, anticipation so urgent it was painful. "Symptoms," Mona had said, "of the mentor condition." That was what Mona called it, "the mentor condition," and before Christmas she had given Annie literature on the subject—"just to prepare you," she had said.

The mentor condition, Annie had read, consisted of an intense relationship between a young protégée (generally female) and a teacher (male, generally married). Perfectly normal, good for the male's ego, and potentially inspiring to the protégée—so long as it was kept under control. Young women who saw the liaison in its proper light, the articles said, could well go on to greatness and a happy life, retaining affectionate ties with their mentors; those who lost perspective were trapped, doomed to a second-hand, lonely future. Control was the key. Cultivate detachment.

So now, when her own hand shook, when sweat started out, Annie would register the emotion and then allow it to run its course—since, once registered, it was by definition under control. At least by her definition. The point was not restraint but awareness. She allowed herself the anxious excitement, the perspiration, the loss of appetite, as if by granting the symptoms of helpless love she wouldn't have to worry about denying herself that love.

Faker, she thought as she chewed a nail to calm the hand down. As if you could deny it—as if you wanted to.

Shampoo. She found a small plastic container under the wash basin and squeezed some shampoo into it. She could wash her hair when she showered in the morning—after a night of love-making it would hang limp against her neck. Next to the vial was a purse-sized aerosol of feminine hygiene deodorant which had come in the mail. She tossed it into her purse.

One side effect of her control tactics was the importance everything had assumed. Conversations with Philip, the food they ate, the places and positions they found themselves in, the look on his face and the look she imagined on hers—these things had begun to imprint themselves on her memory before they had quite passed, so that there was a running catalogue of images which corresponded exactly to the course of her desire. She made a point of spelling things out until they had become part of her, of Annie's life, which Annie could navigate. Unrecognized, they changed: something in them snowed her under.

So, now, with the hygiene deodorant. By throwing it into the purse she had made a decision to spray herself with lavender an hour or so before. Already, one moment of the night confirmed.

She dialed the theater department and got her assistant. "Ellen," she said. "Listen, I can't be at rehearsal tonight. You'll have to tell George."

"He won't be happy. He wants a complete crew tonight."

"Yeah, I don't blame him." George was the director, new this year and imperious. But like the rest of the theater department, he expected inconstancy and required no devious explanations. In fact, the truth would be just vague enough to suit. "I've got to go into L.A." Annie said. "But I've made appointments to fit all the actors, and he can see the costumes anytime."

"L.A. What a drag."

"So tell George I'll be in touch the minute I'm back." Going into Los Angeles covered everything from sick relatives to rendezvous, and for some reason no one ever questioned the phrase.

With the icebox door open Annie poured herself a glass of orange juice and sliced a piece of salami. Then, taking an apple and a box of raisins as well, she moved out to the porch. Students were just getting out of their ten o'clock classes—from her vantage point she could watch them scurry across the parking lot. Today they amused her, with their heavy books and their cowboy clothes. She watched Dave Prince, the one Mona had thought she could be "closer to," trot across the parking lot. The clean brown hair she had trimmed for him bounced against his ears. She started to call out to him, then she realized he would come up and see the packed bag and wonder. The more lies avoided, the better. She chewed on the salami and cracked the apple with her front teeth.

Not long before the appointed time, she walked quickly across the street and the parking lot to the Union. Swinging the bag like a briefcase full of papers, she paused only long enough to drop it into Philip's car.

"Hey, Annie." A short, freckled woman from Jack's class came up to her at the snack bar. "Did you finish the reading?"

"Almost. But I'm not going to class today." Why couldn't she just say yes? No one was asking for details.

"Why not?"

"I've got to go into L.A."

"Stinkers. I hate that city."

Annie sat in a swivel chair and opened *Being and Time*. Fat books were a sure guard against people coming to talk. She sipped her coffee slowly, glancing at the clock above the relish tray. At 11:58 she tossed the styrofoam cup into the wastebasket, and still pretending to read the book, she walked slowly out to the lot. The sun had broken through the haze, but the air in the shade was still cool. As she saw Philip approach from the far side of Weymouth Hall, she waited. He was walking with Urban Whittaker, but Urban, always discreet, turned onto the quad when he saw Annie. She shivered once as Philip came close, a fraction closer than custom allowed, and the thought visited her mind one last time: Will we be able to go back?

Chapter 2

OSCILLATION

At 7:00 A.M. the Santa Monica beach is both at its loveliest and at its most ugly. The sand is cold from the night, and the Pacific brings in a sleepy, cold gray tide. The breeze, soft and salty, riffles the mounded sand and brings in the chatter of gulls. It also lifts the scraps of paper, old tickets, newspapers, and candy wrappers dropped on the parking lot. It leaves the beer cans, bottles, and half-eaten hot dogs choked with sand. But with all its debris the beach is loveliest at dawn because it is only then, before the cleanup crew and crowds arrive, that it regains some of its old

wildness, in the morning chill and in the kelp and fish skeletons deposited by the night tide.

The sun was just up at seven; its rays had not yet struck the beach. Annie buttoned her sweater, turned up the collar, and strode out to the water. The beach was wide, so wide that the water's edge was invisible from the boardwalk, and after wading through sand for five minutes she found she had just reached the top of the rise, at least a hundred yards from the tide line. She sat down and put her arms around her shins, then rubbed her feet, which were numb. She picked at a callus on the ball of one foot and noticed that both feet had picked up tar. She didn't like her feet—they were too wide and always dirty. A pair of joggers went thumping by at the ocean's edge, followed by another with his dog, an Irish setter who ran circles around him and barked impatiently as he padded steadily along. Thump, thump.

"Hey, honey!" called out a fourth runner, a short, square man with a gleaming bald head and probably high blood pressure, "Come gimme some artificial mouth-to-mouth!" Annie laughed and dug her nose into her knees, against the wind. In a little while she would go back to the motel, wash her hair, pack her things, and wait for Philip. Now she wanted only to sit on the cold sand, watch the yellow strip at the horizon approach the shore, and notice things. She wanted to notice everything.

He hadn't wanted her to get up, but she had known that when the space he left cooled down she would be restless and unhappy. "Can't we have breakfast in our room?" she had asked, her fingers on his back as he sat on the side of the bed wiping sleep from his eyes and face. When he had opened the shades, the light filtered through the thin drapes like sand, and she burrowed under the pillow.

"I don't think this is that kind of establishment."

So she had thrown on last night's blouse and a wrinkled skirt and stumbled out with him into the dawn and the traffic. Nowhere on this strip of motels and stereo stores could they find a breakfast place. Nothing was open but the round Orange Julius across the street. Finally they crossed, stopping on the median between lights, and he ordered a double burger and coffee from the boy at the grill. Sitting at the wooden table under the awning, they grinned sleepily at each other. The skin on his face looked heavy after sleeping, and a drop of blood from shaving had dried on his jaw. "Don't you want anything?" he had asked. "Women are supposed to be hungry after sex."

"I'm probably famished, but I'm too tired to know it. We didn't get a lot of sleep."

"That's why I'm hungry."

He looked like an academic in his gray sports jacket and pressed pants, but there was nothing of the classroom in his eyes. She reddened. "This should be some lecture you give."

"It won't be any good at all. I'm too distracted. I'll try to make it amusing." He glanced at his watch and gulped his coffee. "Here, you finish this."

"No, thanks."

And then he had left to give his speech, brisk and motivated. She had wished for an instant to have stayed in bed—it had been a romantic letdown for the long night to end in a sidewalk-stand breakfast. But it had been funny too. As are most things with us, she had thought as he drove off. The only thing that's sad and not funny is how I love him. But just then that hadn't seemed sad.

The sand was damp. Dew had stolen through the back of Annie's skirt and when she tried to brush the tiny grains off, they stuck and smeared. She struggled back over the beach to the motel, flat and ugly in the daylight. "The Sea Gull," the sign read, with a silhouette of a roosting bird. They had paid twenty-five dollars in advance, and while Philip was pulling bills out of his wallet the manager had undressed her with his eyes. The room had turquoise lamps on either side of the bed, a foldaway couch, and a Formica coffee table. The bed, soft but big, squatted in the middle. "King-size!" Annie had said when they first opened the door. "It's actually *made* for two people!"

They had lain on top of the bedspread for a while with their clothes on. Annie had put her head on Philip's hip and he had stroked her breasts, but she had felt self-conscious and, for the first time, stereotyped. It was embarrassing to do this, to find a sleazy motel for an illlicit fuck. Joking about the torn turquoise spread hadn't helped. They had gone for drinks.

Now she knew the answer. They could not be as before. Even if nothing changed, if she just continued to come into Los Angeles the afternoon he taught there while he kept coming to her place on Tuesdays, it would be wholly different.

For one thing, the control was slipping away. Annie had felt herself losing it as they walked down the street in Westwood. People had turned to look at them, but not because they were beautiful or exotic, and they had developed a habitual constraint in public. It's the connection, Annie thought—the blood rushes into the capillaries and quickens at a touch, and it radiates something people want to have rubbed off on them. It was why people gathered around them at the college, why they devoured them. Annie couldn't see herself in this state, but she saw it reflected in Philip, and it alarmed and excited her at once.

She drank martinis now with him, loving the cool, clean taste of the gin after the rot wine and grass at school. It had been happy hour in the bar; the waitress had brought them extra drinks, and Annie had grown warm and giddy. Floating high in the smoke of the room, she had pulled away from herself until another Annie seemed to stand behind Philip, facing her, watching. As Philip talked about his UCLA class, she found herself turning to this imaginary voyeur and telling her a dream from the night before:

Philip and I were in a crowded room, she had explained silently to the watching Annie. *We were both sitting in an overstuffed armchair, but we couldn't touch because of the people. Everyone we knew was there, his family too, and they all suspected us. Suddenly we started to make love in the chair. But I knew they were all staring at us and I felt ashamed.*

She told herself the dream because the bar had become like the room in the dream, and all she wanted was to climb into the big leather chair with Philip. But only their hands could reach across the oak table, and in the candlelight she watched their fingers touch.

"What do you want to do?" Philip had asked. "Do you want dinner?"

"Not really. Do you?"

"No. Do you want to see a movie?"

"All right."

"You don't care."

"No. It would be nice, if it's a nice movie."

They had gone to the movie, a bittersweet comedy about a divorced woman who finds new love. They had kissed at odd moments and stayed almost to the end, when Philip leaned over and asked, "Are you ready for bed?"

"I want to be there now. I can't stand it."

Philip had pulled onto the freeway and driven fast toward the beach. The turquoise room waited for them, with its print of Oaxaca on the wall and its bed like a ship on the turquoise sea.

"Let me undress you," said Annie. "I haven't undressed you in ages."

"All right."

She sat on his belly and unbuttoned his shirt, massaging his neck and chest with its mat of gray hair. After she had pulled off the shirt, she turned and worked at his belt while he strayed over her back and thighs. She leaned into his scrotum, which looked both hard and soft and smelled very sweet, and she did not suck but let her mouth slide all over. Then he was turning her around, and they were both shy, at a distance on the bed, hesitant. He knelt with her legs around his waist, then put his hand cautiously in between them, as if deciding what to do. Lifting her legs high over her head then and shifting her pelvis, he went in with his mouth and slowly the gentleness heated up, and he murmured, "Sweet," and bit and pulled at her while she clutched at his back and felt the rivers begin to run over her breasts and down into her thighs. They moved quickly, pitching about on the bed, and sometimes when Annie opened her eyes in the dark she didn't know where she was or what part of his body was in her mouth or between her legs. Then he entered her, with the whole force of his age, and the violence pierced and rolled and cracked open and fell, spilling outward and still tearing through them. With his arms under her knees, her sex faced him like a fountainhead, and she leaped into him as he came, a shuddering come and then another, and then they lay still and sweating.

They slept. He slipped out finally, and Annie woke once or twice in his arms, and he mumbled.

Or maybe they did not sleep, but only held there in a kind of trance until they unlocked. He woke her with his cock, big again.

"How does that feel?"

"Good. Teasing, but good. How long can you keep this up?"

"Forever, I think." But he couldn't, and they came again, sleepier this time, while dawn came in a rush over their damp bodies.

Returning from the beach, Annie found a doughnut shop open down the street. It smelled of grease and sugar; behind the counter a fat woman drummed her fingers impatiently. "A buttermilk twist," Annie finally said, not really wanting one. She took the bag with the doughnut and coffee back to the room. Opening *Being and Time,* she ate and tried to read, but occasionally she looked up and saw the bed—the maid hadn't been in yet—and her muscles went weak. There, staring her in the face, was the cause and reason for her present life—and there, turning the page, it was nothing, and she was calmly breakfasting and laboring through a dead man's philosophy. Of that devastating sensation and of the things around her—the book, the greasy roll, the lamp—one had to exist and the other be a sort of trick. Usually the ordinary things were just an outline, a front made up of eating, sleeping, working. But sometimes it seemed plain that the strange, sweet passion was no more than that, a thing which passed while all the rest went on. Annie didn't like this second feeling—it was a cold way of looking, a way of giving up. It was also a more enduring vision than the first, and she thought it was probably closer to truth. Then the rush came again and she could feel Philip exploding inside her,

the tremor sounding through her blood. It came so close, that
way, to being enough.

Before he opened the motel door, Philip stopped a moment to
study Annie through the window. She was perched on the side of
the couch, her legs curled neatly under her, her cigarette left to
burn in the ashtray. Her sharp face was intent on the book, while
occasionally she bit at a hangnail on her thumb. Almost no one,
he thought, would see her as rare. Attractive, maybe sexy, intelligent and fun. Not beautiful. They would not recognize her walk,
the swing of her legs from the hip. He thought of the way she
bent down, the seconds she took before answering a question,
finally couching her gravest thoughts in an attempt at wit. Few
would care about the curve that ran up her slender thigh and
around her hip, especially as she sat now. He loved that curve.

But they had to get going. There was no time to take her back
to bed, as he would have liked to, just to stroke a single one of
her limbs, to remind himself it was there.

He dropped her off at the railroad tracks behind the school,
and they glanced around before they kissed quickly. "Are you
going to class?" he asked.

"No. Are you?"

"I told Urban to substitute."

She pulled her bag out of the back seat. "Thanks, mister—it's
been real fun!"

"Yeah, sweetheart, I'll stop by when I'm in town again!"

Grinning, Philip drove away. In the rear-view mirror he saw
Annie sit down for a minute on the tracks, as if she were suddenly
dizzy, or too tired to walk. He stopped at a light and watched her
until, just as suddenly, she rose and walked briskly toward the
school, like a traveler headed for an appointment that cannot
wait.

When Annie got back to her place there was a note taped to the
door: *Call me, Mona.* She left the note there and went in, letting

her suitcase drop to the floor. Her first instinct was to hide. She could go to the library, or to the costume studio and lock the door. Mona would think she hadn't seen the note. That would give her a few hours' reprieve. But the note might have been left last night, and surely Annie wouldn't go to either of those places without stopping here first. Besides, she never went to the library; besides, Mona would check the studio; besides, she had told Ellen she was going to L.A. and would be back.

She sank into the green chair. This was absurd. She had no earthly reason to run from Mona—Mona was her only friend. She saw little enough of her as it was these days, without avoiding her as one would an ex-lover.

With all her new understandings, Annie had ceased to understand Mona, and she did not want Mona to have the power of seeing her confused. There had been other notes, like this, asking Annie to call, and there had been long sessions in the ample sitting room at Mona's house, full of belittlings from Mona and of Annie's attempts to scale their friendship like an icy slope, sliding ever back. Last time they met, Annie had thought, *It's the passion.* That had been the gap in all Mona's old stories—she didn't want Annie to know the passion. "You're always happy," Mona had said accusingly, that time.

"How do you know? Maybe I cry myself to sleep at night."

"No, you're always happy. But it won't last forever. I was happy with Bruce too, you know."

"Sometimes I think you want him back."

"Sometimes I think I do too," Mona had begun to admit, then she had caught herself. "But it was over when it started—when he left his wife. That's something you ought to think about. What'll happen to her, if you get him to leave her?"

You think you know everything, Annie had said to herself, then aloud, "Philip's not leaving his wife."

"But don't you want him to?"

"No. It's not like that." *Ask why,* Annie had wanted to challenge her. *Ask how I'm free.*

Mona had only shaken her head and said she didn't get it; then they had discussed Clyde. Annie was sick of being accused and she was sick of talking about Clyde. Once, they had made a date for tennis, but instead of playing they had just skipped ahead to the sauna and the wine. When they talked, now, their talk came short and breathy, as if they kept stumbling over something.

But damn it, Annie thought, I need you. She peeled the note off the door. I counted on you. I hadn't planned to go this one alone. She shut the door and, leaning back against it, studied her apartment. She had made some improvements since Philip had started coming over, but it was still hopelessy dingy. How happy she'd been, in August, when she had found her own place! It was a door she could shut in everyone's face, even Mona's—a cocoon she could wrap around herself, to proceed with the messy business of growth until a butterfly had emerged, wild and translucent. Maybe Philip had unfolded the wings of the butterfly, she couldn't be sure. But she had to discard the cocoon, her hiding place, her solitude, as a relic.

Just so, she had to call Mona. Selfishly, she thought their friendship could be a relic too, which threatened to crumble when exposed to air. As if to stave off the threat, she put on her need of Mona like a tattered coat as she picked up the phone. But while she snapped out the numbers it was "Philip" she whispered to herself, turning the *l* over with her tongue. Phi*l*ip. It steadied her as the phone rang—Philip, like a charm, his name filling the room.

Mona's house was a neat Victorian, grayish-blue edged in white, repainted every other year by the landlady. The six women who lived in it were all theater students, who dramatized their domestic lives by either loving one another intensely or refusing to speak. Behind their large and exuberant gestures Annie sensed tension, a fear of betrayal. They had asked her to join them in the house last year, but she had said no, she'd found a place. She had wanted her dark nest, her solitude. Here, the rooms were always full of air and light from the bay windows, full of well-trained singing voices and melodramatic quarrels, and sometimes Annie was jealous. All that life, right at hand.

As she approached she saw one of Mona's roommates hoist herself into a shoulder stand on the front porch. Somewhere on the third story someone was rehearsing *Lear*. Mona's room was up one flight, at the back, where French windows led out to the balcony. She and Bruce had sold most of their furniture after they divorced, but Mona had taken the velvet hangings and the handwoven bedspread and the bookcase Bruce had carved and given her. Except for Clyde's books and clothes and the pair of skis standing in the corner, there was no sign that someone else lived here too.

Mona was sitting on the bed eating a yogurt and listening to Ravel. "Have you seen Clyde?" she asked.

"No. Should I have?"

"You will. He always runs to you when he can't understand me."

It had been true, once or twice. Clyde had come by looking like a whipped dog, and Annie had sworn Mona's love and need for him. It had been the need that worked. "What did you do to him this time?"

"I threw a chair at him in rehearsal last night. I'm surprised you haven't heard. He thought I'd gone nuts. He's been telling everybody to check my pockets for sleeping pills and to tell me how nice I am. God knows where he spent the night."

"So tell me why you did it."

"He's not a virgin." Mona sounded tired of the subject. "I mean, he wasn't. Before me. He fucked someone named Sylvia all last year. And Christ knows, before that."

"And?" There had to be more to this, Annie thought.

"And don't you see? When I met him—after being married, after Bruce and all that—I thought he was so *pure*. I handled him like a piece of rare glass."

"You were happy with him in bed."

"Of course I was. It was good—I *made* it good. I'd never been with a virgin before. It was terribly important for it to be *right*. I taught him—oh, so carefully! How to make love, how to give, all that bullshit!" Mona had got up from the bed and was walking around the room, crossing and uncrossing her arms. Annie resisted the urge to smile; this was not supposed to be funny.

"So why'd he tell you? How did it come up?"

"His conscience. He said it was weighing on his conscience. And it's not like he'd just been deflowered—oh, no! They used to do it in her dorm room, every night, while her roommate was supposedly asleep. Asleep! Oh, the whole thing revolts me. I don't want to talk about it."

Annie couldn't take Clyde's side; she didn't like him. Clyde was a diplomat's son, schooled in the pretense of innocence. Now, he wandered in a fog like a prodigal, hovering around the light that was Mona, but later he would work his way home, and once safely there he wouldn't care if her light flickered or died. He would naturally lie, out of selfishness and fear—but Annie had to point out that the falsehood had taken place six months before. "It was almost an act of courage to admit it now, wasn't it? He must have known he was taking a risk."

"But that's just the point! It wasn't just one lie he told me a long time ago. It's been false every day from the start. Every time we made love, every time I touched him, I thought of him as virginal! Not consciously, but for me he was *untouched*. That's why he told me he'd never had sex before. He wanted me to think that way. He knew I couldn't resist purity."

Poor Clyde, Annie thought. You should never have said anything.

"It's over, anyway, "Mona said. "You can just tell him that, if he asks. It's dead. I'm not patient with betrayal. I'm just waiting for him to come get his crap out of here. You can have the key to your apartment back."

"Oh, keep it. At least till he's really gone." Mona didn't argue. Annie got up and turned the record over. The other side was Debussy. Mona's pile rug, deep and comforting, kissed the soles of her feet as she walked back.

"Where were you yesterday, anyway?" Mona asked. "I tried to call you, but Ellen said you'd gone to the city."

"Yeah, I went in with Philip. He teaches a class there."

And you stayed the night?"

"Uh-huh."

Mona lit a Tiparillo, the kind they had smoked last year. The plastic tip looked hard and tasteless as she drew in the smoke, inhaling slightly. Annie waited for her to rip the delicate web spun in the night, but Mona only sighed and, pressing her fingers to the bridge of her nose, shook her head. "It's awful," she said, "that we accept things so easily. And then a slight break, and the whole wall just collapses." She dropped her hand and looked up at Annie. "We're consumed with the self," she said.

"Maybe."

"So how was it, in L.A.?"

"It was terrific."

A shadow came over Mona's face. Annie wanted to go to her, to pour girlishly forth as Mona had just done; but even as she took another step over the pile rug, that shadow repelled her. "Really terrific," she repeated. And before Mona could pierce her battlement, Annie had deflected her with excuses, assurances, and goodbyes. She skipped down the steps of the broad front porch, moving fast to keep up with the beat of her heart.

◇   ◇   ◇   ◇   ◇   ◇   ◇   ◇   ◇

The clock above the counter at the restaurant read 12:15 as Philip worked his way over to the group in the corner. He noticed that Urban Whittaker had already distributed an agenda for the noon meeting, and Jack was pouring beer.

"Glad you could make it, Phil," Urban said without looking up.

"Held up by a student, I guess." Keith Clarke squinted at him through thick glasses which sat crooked on his thin nose and distorted his eyes. Keith was a professional linguist, but he reminded Philip of a high school chemistry buff, the kind who took the prize on *Whiz Kids*.

"No, I had a long-distance phone call."

Philip detested these meetings. Instead of holding court in the office or in a seminar room, the department chose tacky lunch places like this one, Ronnie's Pizza, with its chipped Formica tables and globular hanging lamps. They got a pitcher of beer and pretended it was a social occasion, and they were proud of themselves for foiling the unwritten law that meetings should be dull, dreary affairs.

But the meetings were not only dull but inconvenient. Urban always tried to draw up some plan on a piece of paper or a napkin because he lacked a blackboard; as Jack's nerves acted up he drank too much and belched; beer and ketchup stained the notes. Nothing was ever accomplished. Urban always forgot what it was they had decided and had to come around the next day to reconstruct the proposal and get each member's opinion. Betty, the secretary, refused to spend her lunch hour in a bar or cafeteria, taking down minutes, and Philip didn't blame her. The smell of the places was bad enough to distract him from administrative concerns—he just wanted fresh air and peace.

"Hey, let's get a pizza," Jack said, and before anyone could answer he called the waitress. "Pepperoni and onion, large."

"I hate onions," said Keith.

"Don't get grease on this memo," Urban added. "It's from the president's office. They want a speaker for the alumni meeting in Pasadena. Stan, why don't you go talk about your book?"

"We gave them a speaker last time," said Jack. "Why don't they go pick on the history people?"

"I'd, uh, rather not talk about the book right now, Urban, if you don't mind," said Stan Weiner, their ethical philosopher, from somewhere deep in his large, sunken chest. "It's still, uh, in a state of flux, if you know what I mean."

"He's on page ten," Jack whispered too loudly to Philip, and Stan turned red and stared at the table.

What a bunch of kids we are, thought Philip. Boys, the philosophy boys. He wished there were a woman in the department, to make it less a stag group. But if she were beautiful, he thought, I'd be after her, and so would Urban and probably Jack. If she were ugly, she'd be my only friend, and they'd treat her like a freak.

Keith would hate her either way, for being female, and Stan's wife would be endlessly inviting her to tea and asking about her personal life. It would be impossible for her no matter what.

As he poured himself a beer Philip examined his imaginary colleague and suddenly realized he was seeing Annie Redfield. The role could be hers, if she wanted it. She could handle these boys. And so stay at Newhall. What fantasy.

Urban's voice droned on. The pizza came, and Keith began to argue with his mouth full of pepperoni. Six teenagers had come in with a transistor, and the professors had to shout to hear one another. Philip poured himself another beer and refilled Urban's glass. "What do you think?" Urban asked him.

"About what?"

"About these room assignments?"

"I think we ought to adjourn. We're all getting deaf and hoarse."

"We haven't finished the pizza!" shouted Jack.

"It's a lousy pizza," said Stan.

"Look, we're not getting anything done here," Philip said. "Let's meet tomorrow." He wanted to drive up the mountain and locate Joan. She would be at the bird observatory, drawing up charts or leading a group of school children through the displays. Or else the people at the station would tell him she was in the field, and he would have to track down the '67 VW she insisted on driving. With luck he would find her two hundred yards from the car, alone, crouched behind a bush and peering out over the valley with her binoculars. A far more satisfying occupation, he thought, than his own. He would tug her away from it and then take her out to dinner tonight. Didi was home from school, sick of books and looking for work, so she could stay with Emily. No, he would take them all out, to cheer Didi up—but this afternoon, while the girls were out of the house, he would bring Joan home and to bed. Yes.

"Look," said Urban, "there are *things* we've *got* to *decide*." He tapped on the table for emphasis and glared at Philip. Urban did not like to have his plans altered or his power usurped.

The transistor walked out. "Okay. Let's go on," Philip said wearily. "I'm sorry." The fantasy of Joan vanished. She would leave the observatory before he got there anyway, or be impossible to find in the mountains. Didi might give up pounding the pavement and come home at any time, and Emily had to be picked up by three.

He wondered why he should have imagined Annie as a professor. She didn't belong to this world—her vocation lay outside. To envision her remaining here, wasting her energies and her talent, was to point out what he already knew about himself. Through her eyes he surveyed the company at the table: he found Urban a bore, Keith a manipulator, Stan a hypocrite, Jack greedy and narcissistic. With degrees from Harvard, Columbia, Yale, they were transplants from the East, mixing locker-room talk with their textbook conversations. And among them he was no better. *A tenured position in a small elite private college . . . an academic career, brilllant* in a minor sort of way . . . *lionized by publishers . . . adaptable wife . . . affairs with exceptional female students.* Well, what else did one do? Even if he could begin again, he would go the same way.

Annie knew there was more to him, that thus far he had fallen short. It was easy for her—all was still potential, and she could wrap her unknown future like a cloak around her failures. For him there had been no hiding since Annie had found him out; all his lukewarm achievements, his shortcuts, stood exposed,

The meeting broke up. Jack was stuffing cold pizza into a doggie bag. Urban leaned toward Philip. His breath was heavy. "Can you stop by my place, just for a minute?" he asked.

"Sure." They walked out together. An east wind had sprung up, pushing a bank of clouds across the sky, and Philip forecast with pleasure that it would finally rain.

As he pulled up in front of Urban's neat adobe house, the wind riffled through the bougainvillea clinging to the fence and

sprayed red petals over the broad walk. "Hush, you!" a voice called from inside as Urban's wire terrier yapped at Philip's heels. Harriet was home. He saw her looking sternly through the blinds at the dog and then lighting a cigarette before coming to answer the door.

Harriet was always home, and she was always dressed, as now, in a flowered housedress, or in knit slacks that hugged her bottom, pushing the cheeks in to obliterate the crevice between them. Once, Harriet had had a good figure. When Urban first brought her down from Seattle she had worn a bouffant hairstyle and heels that must have pinched but had made her legs look terrific. She and Urban used to give lots of nonacademic parties, with insurance people and the grounds crew from the college and ex-government people in trouble with McCarthy—all very democratic. Harriet would get drunk and sing corny songs, and afterward she would pull Joan into the kitchen with her to cry. She had cried because her husband was going to be unfaithful to her, because her figure would melt away, because life and bravery would desert her, and because she understood it all and couldn't stop any of it.

"You're bleeding," she said matter-of-factly to Philip as she opened, picking red petals from his lapels. "Rupert, get down."

"Oh, he's all right."

"How're the girls? Hear from Didi?"

"She's home. Taking a break from the campus scene."

"No concentration, kids today."

She didn't ask about Joan. A dozen years had passed since Joan had sat in the kitchen and listened to her, and all Harriet's premonitions had come true, so she hardly spoke to Joan anymore. People needed a confidante; they told you their secrets, then they held your knowledge against you. Joan had mourned when Harriet stopped speaking to her. Now Harriet was a hypochondriac and talked, Philip supposed, to doctors—he was glad not to be one. Urban thought she should have an affair.

As if she'd read his thoughts, Harriet turned abruptly back to the kitchen. "Urban's upstairs," she said through her cigarette.

Sitting at the small desk in his study with his back to the door and smoking a cigar, Urban looked like a petty Napoleon. Cigar smoke filled the room, and Philip coughed. "Would you mind closing the door?" Urban said without turning around.

"Yes, I would, unless you open a window or put that thing out."

Urban pushed at the window latch. Outside, the wind had quieted and a drizzle had begun. Philip shut the door and sat down.

Urban swung his chair around. "There are two things we've got to talk about," he said. "The first is Jack."

They were this way with each other—blunt and simple, but with an edge underneath. Philip didn't want to be close to this man, and Urban was sharp enough to discern the judgment passed. "What about Jack?" Philip asked.

"Well, he's on the verge of a breakdown."

"That's an exaggeration."

"Maybe—I don't know. But the president has been getting negative reports, from students and from faculty. He wants us to grant Jack a medical leave."

"What sort of reports?"

"A student on a tutorial says that she reads her papers aloud to him in his office while he stares at the newspaper. The want ads, the race results—he clips coupons, for God's sake. Existentialism is supposed to meet once a week. There are fifteen weeks in the semester. He cancels class three times, gives them a take-home final over the holidays, and tells them not to come to class in January. These kids' parents pay an average of eighty bucks for a three-hour class—that's twelve hundred dollars they're paying each semester for nothing! More, when you realize he's almost quit lecturing and just lets them shoot bull all evening. When he does lecture, he gets carried away and starts to shout until he's almost incoherent. That's what the president's been hearing."

"I've heard some of it too. But he won't take a leave."

"It's up to us to persuade him."

"Oh, Christ." Philip pictured the talks over late-night drinks at some expensive bar, with Jack never picking up the tab. He pictured the endless arguments, the wheedling, the distrust, the dull conferences, like this one, with Urban. He got up—if he had to talk this out, at least he didn't have to sit still. "Who's been complaining about him? Reliable people? If he does need a break, why doesn't somebody talk to Ruth, or to his psychiatrist? They have a lot more influence over him than we do."

"They also don't know what's happening to his classes. Besides, the president doesn't want anyone to get this wrong, to think we're trying to push out a tenured professor. If Jack decides to tell them that's his business, but we can't leak it."

" 'Leak it'? You make this sound like the CIA." Philip pushed the window open further; the rain had started to come down in earnest, and a few drops landed on his hand. "Anyway, you know it'll get out somehow, and then it'll be a scandal instead of a normal proceeding."

"Don't get yourself worked up." Urban sat and watched him move. Urban liked to sit. He would sit immobile in a stiff wooden chair through a long, stuffy convocation. He sat as if rooted to the ground through the chair, his buttocks spread neatly over the seat.

"Sorry."

"Let me tell you the second part of this. It isn't about Jack—it has to do with me. As you know, Harriet and I haven't been hitting it off too well lately. She—we, rather—thought maybe a change would help." Urban stubbed out his cigar and started to clean his fingernails. "I don't know when it started—maybe you could tell, from the outside. I've grown too used to this existence. I give her money, she gives me a home. I screw around on her, she makes life intolerable. Inertia sets in. We both get fat." He chuckled. "And we thought we were so unusual."

Philip had sat down. Against his will, he felt sympathy which he couldn't express. "I know what you mean," he said ineffectually.

"No, you don't. Harriet doesn't get involved in things, like Joan. She's more . . . ordinary. And I'm not like you. But the point is I want it to work out. I'm willing to do whatever has to be done for it to work out. Neither of us has given up, not entirely. Can you understand that?"

Philip guessed he could, as much as he could understand couples who fought, hoping despite reality to change one another, as Urban and Harriet did. He believed in his heart that he accepted his wife, mostly because he thought about her so little. He could vaguely remember the epiphanic point in his past when he had noticed her in some daily pose and had realized with relief, *I don't have to think about you. You are there.*

"So," he said to Urban, his impatience rising against this hope of conjugal change, "you want to take a leave too. You're not up for one."

"The president says I can take it without pay." Urban hadn't looked up from his fingernails, which were bright pink without a speck of dirt. "That is, if someone will chair the department in my stead, and if you'll put off your sabbatical. I want you to do both."

"Ah." Philip had missed Urban's point. He hadn't thought about his leave in weeks. Joan was waiting on her grant, Didi talked only of getting a job. But somehow, he had thought, they would all fly off, and once there, he would be good to them, wonderfully good. "I don't owe you any favors, Urban," he said.

"Just the fall semester, Phil. Harriet and I could disappear to Florida or somewhere, where there wouldn't be department meetings—"

"Or other women."

"Yes, but I'm too old for that anyway. I should quit. So should you."

Philip let the remark pass. "My family's been looking forward to this, Urban. I'm not free to decide for them, you know. Emily's ripe for the experience."

"It's just a semester. The time as chair would give you more travel money." Urban lit a cigar and blinked his small eyes. "And I thought there might, well, be advantages to you in staying."

"Such as?"

"I wouldn't know."

He meant Annie. Philip could hardly pretend it was a secret. That fantasy, of her staying on at Newhall, was the reason he hadn't focused on England these last weeks, hadn't prepared the syllabus or scheduled speakers for the conference. If he were determined to go, he needed only to refuse Urban, to whom he owed nothing. But Annie would be gone when he returned. Staying, he could hold her here, somehow, for just a few months more. He knew he could.

He should say no, immediately. "I'll have to think about it, Urban," he said. "I'll have to talk it over with Joan. She and the girls are awfully eager to go."

"And are you?"

"Oh, I'm about the same anywhere. You know that."

They let the conversation wander, let each other retreat, and then Philip left. He promised to come to a decision soon.

Pulling out of Urban's subdivision onto the commercial strip that led out of town, Philip stopped at a bar and ordered a double martini. He was given neither to self-analysis nor to self-deception. He would not cancel England for Urban's sake, and certainly not for Jack, whose sanity looked in danger whether in or out of the classroom. Yet he had said he might cancel, to stay at Newhall. If he was falling in love, nothing about it was right and the thing had to stop. And what had "love" to do with his condition? Psychologists generally narrowed symptoms of love down to certain physical sensations, sensations he wasn't feeling now.

Nietzsche: *Love is at bottom the hatred between the sexes.* Goddamn it, stop thinking, he said to himself as the drink came. It tasted good; he ate the olive and asked for a glass of water and matches. Who cared what Nietzsche thought? Philip could never turn off his mind, his analytic faculty—a product of thinking too long about too many things. He thought how a young person would add, "and not enough feeling," but this was not so. He only went over all that he felt; his mind worked away behind the emotions and made connections where he wanted none. Now, having introduced the subject of love, he found himself dwelling on Harriet Whittaker. She was a shrill, nervous woman whose marriage was on the rocks—but she had thrived on being with Urban in a crowd, and he doubted she sincerely wanted her husband alone on a second honeymoon at this point. While that would be easy for Urban, it would not accomplish her purpose. As Philip pondered it, the leave seemed to be entirely Urban's idea.

But he didn't want to think about Urban and Harriet. What, then? Schopenhauer: *The mind's ideas are arranged and selected by the will. The will is first cause.* He would elect to think of Joan, of Didi and Emily. Joan needed a break, more than he did, from the constant frustration of her work. Didi might not want Berkeley, but he couldn't let her slide back to Newhall. And Emily deserved at least a few months' unstinting attention, which he could not give her here.

And there was England. Replete with memories, the image of England crept up on him, as he slowly convinced himself of the need to return there. He should get out of the smog; he smoked enough cigarettes without needing to breathe carbon monoxide as well. They could rent a house near Salisbury, where Emily would go to school and probably take on an accent. He would study birds with Joan in Cornwall and take Didi fishing at the lakes. He did love England, especially in the fall. The clouds cracked open and the leaves turned an abrupt red in October; then the frost came flashing in a month later. He pictured the Cotswolds in September and could almost smell the damp yellow leaves and rich decay. He had seen his first red-breasted fly-catcher there, with Joan, right after their marriage. She had been sprightly then. The English loved her in her tweeds and brogues and would laugh as she clapped at a covey of quail which shot out of the brush by their feet. At night they had made love on the hard floor by their fireplace, one side of their bodies roasting, the other in the cold like the dark side of the moon. Damn it, he said mentally to Urban, my marriage isn't all honeymoon either. It could use some restoration.

Urban: *But who are you harming now? And you're probably doing the girl some good.* Freud: *The father-daughter attraction, its benefits*

*and pitfalls. How much good we do them, how they grow when sexu-
ally involved with an experienced man.* Hogwash. He wasn't teaching Annie a thing. She wasn't growing but becoming neurotic.

He hated thinking like this. Why had he even considered the
idea of staying? Annie called June "the end"—she was leaving, to
seek her fortune. Still, she would stay if he asked, he was sure of
that. Which was precisely the danger. Someone had to have control. Still (and as he finished the martini it came forcibly on him),
the temptation remained. To stay, to have things just as they were
for a little longer. It had been so short—there was some passion,
he felt sure, unachieved. Another night together—four, five, ten
nights together. England, as Urban had pointed out, would not
sink below the sea, and there would be other conferences.

I think, he thought, like a boy in his first flush. I must not go
on this way. He saw at once and clearly the effect Annie was
having on his life. It was strange he hadn't noticed it before, as if
he had had some kind of immunity. It was March now—if he
kept seeing her, by June the choice would be made for him.
Regardless of Urban or Jack or Joan, he would in June decide to
stay. Eventually the affair would take over his marriage and his
life, and he and Annie would be living guiltily together while she
bloomed and he grew old. And then she would wither, his
Annie—whom he could not have and make happy at the same
time. For that matter he couldn't make her happy now, except in
bed. He had watched her in public, anxious, overly vivacious,
yearning. He swore at Urban Whittaker for making it all so
obvious. The thing must end, not in a few months but now. He
had to think of his family and of the best thing to do.

Philip ordered a beer chaser, but felt no thirst when it came.
He had a great hunger for Annie suddenly, for her long body
cupped in his arms on her small bed with white sheets. He
wanted to watch her face turn, beads of sweat on her upper lip as
he rode her; he wanted to bury his head between her legs. He left
the beer and a five-dollar bill on the table. He dialed, his fingers
like jelly. She was home.

◇   ◇   ◇   ◇   ◇   ◇   ◇   ◇   ◇

The first thing Annie thought when she saw Didi Decker working at the post office was *two weeks*. Two weeks since he had
called her like that, almost desperate, when she was on her way
out the door, and since that time he had not called or come by at
all. As she edged up in the line to where Didi counted out
stamps, her heart hammered. Two weeks and a day, to be exact—
she counted in half days now, to give each measure of time its
chance. The chances went by just the same, unseized. It was her
turn in line. "Hi!" she said to Didi. "I didn't know *you* were in
town."

"Needed a break from school. I figured I could work a few
months. Hang out a minute, this crowd's almost gone."

Annie got her stamps and stood to the side. She had met
Philip's daughter only once, before Christmas, when Didi had
come to a campus party with her father. Philip had introduced
them and gone off to talk with Jack. "I've heard about you," Didi
had said, and Annie's lips had frozen over her wineglass as the
girl went on. "You're the one who begged my father to be your
adviser because Jack Wheelbright's such a lech."

"Well—"

"Hey, I don't blame you. I grew up with these guys around the
house. Campus brat."

"So you said screw the free tuition at this place and went to
Berkeley."

"Right." Didi's smile had been lopsided, unwilling, like
Philip's.

"What're you studying?"

"Biology. When I study." They had both sunk into a spring-
less, moldy couch. The party had been in a long, low-ceilinged
basement beneath the dining hall, which smelled of fried pota-
toes and tomato sauce. "It'll sound funny, coming from me,"
Didi had said, leaning close, "but I think you're lucky to be
working with my dad. He's one of the few real intellectuals left—
you know, the ones who can actually get excited about it."

That had been barely four months ago, when everything had seemed possible and easy. Annie had drunk in Didi's rough, open looks, her speech, anything that might partake of Philip. Now she leaned against the counter as if she had nothing better to do, watching Didi handle her customers, waiting for a few minutes of idle talk that might yield her a clue.

That last afternoon, Philip had sat with her on the floor, smoking, while he told her how they had to get Jack to take a leave, and how she might listen to what other students were saying about Jack to see how bad the situation really was. "He can be a brilliant teacher, as you know," he had said. "He's got tenure—it'd be hard to fire him—but I don't want him forced. I also don't want him screwing up my sabbatical."

Annie remembered how, after the rain had stopped, the sun had filtered through the live oak and touched the room with warmth. He had had one arm across her thighs, his fingers holding a cigarette, while the ashtray perched precariously on his knee. Then the door had opened, and Mona had started to walk in.

She had called earlier, but in the rush of the afternoon Annie had forgotten. (*Did* I forget? she wondered now.) And she had knocked, some minutes before, but whenever people had knocked Annie had simply lain still against Philip, breathing quietly, and waited for them to go away. And indeed, Mona had left. Then she had changed her mind and returned, carrying her costume for Annie to fix, with the key Annie had told her to keep. When she had pushed open the door and seen Philip, Mona had gone white, while he hid his face like a criminal. Annie remembered jumping up, spilling the ashtray; she had reached the door just as Mona was closing it again. "It's all right," she had said.

"I'm sorry. Oh, Christ, I'm sorry," said Mona, trying to shut herself out.

"Look, it's okay. Call me. We'll talk."

"I didn't mean to. I called, I knocked. Jesus." Mona's wood clogs had clattered on the steps and faded away down the walk.

"It's her costume for Maggie, in *Cat on a Hot Tin Roof*," Annie had explained as she brought the dress in. "The seam's ripped."

Philip had regained his composure and was brushing ashes from his pants. "I'm glad I was dressed," he had said breezily. "Who was that woman?"

"That was Mona. She knows about us."

"She does, does she?"

"It's all right. She has nothing to do with anybody—I mean anybody we know. I've always told her everything."

"What do you mean, 'everything.'?" he had teased. "Do you go into our favorite positions, like Jack does with you?"

"No! As a matter of fact she hasn't wanted to hear much. She was involved with a married man once, and it turned out badly."

"How, badly?"

"She married him."

I shouldn't have told anyone, Annie had thought later, turning in her bed at night. I shouldn't have needed to talk about Philip to anyone but Philip. And she thought maybe that was why he didn't come by. There had to be something. Then she remembered thinking how it was bound to change, after a night in the city together. It was bound to change anyway. But not like this. Not this.

"So how's your thesis going?" Didi asked. The line of customers had evaporated, and other clerks had left their windows.

"Slowly. You're living at home?"

"For now. The rent is right, though I don't know if I can take my mother." She rolled her eyes, and Annie thought of the petite woman with the large sunglasses obscuring her face. Didi had her father's looks, his broad, open features and large bones; she wore no makeup and had pulled her dark blond hair back with a barrette, making her look still more mannish. "There's a baby-sitting catch, too. My dad wants off the hook in the late afternoon when my litle sister's home."

"That's Emily?"

"Yeah. You know her?"

Snub nose and straight California blond hair. After Mona's intrusion, Philip had checked his watch and said he had to run, he was late to pick up Emily. "Take me with you," Annie had asked, not wanting to be left there alone in the room. She expected refusal.

"Okay, get dressed," he had surprised her by saying. "You've got exactly thirty seconds." And they had raced along the freeway to Emily's school, where Emily waited on the grass doing cartwheels. She had done five in a row for Annie, her blond hair spinning over the flat green lawn; then she had shown off her cheerleader routine, with a twig for a baton, flipping it through the air and catching it between her legs. Riding home, she had sat between Annie and Philip in the front seat.

"She's adorable," Annie had said.

He had laughed. "No, not that. A far cry from it." But his eyes glancing down at Emily had spoken otherwise.

"Yeah, I met her once," Annie heard herself saying now. "Cute kid. I guess she'll go to school with the British next year."

"Looks like it."

"And you?"

"I don't know if I'll go. I've got to be home awhile before I know." She fixed Annie with her wide-set eyes, Philip's blue eyes, and Annie's chest constricted. *Know what?* As she let her breath back out it occurred to her that Philip could feel that same panic, with his daughter home; at any moment Didi might find him out. "Tomorrow they start me on a delivery route—it's what I applied for," Didi was going on. "What's your address?"

"Twenty-six East Fourth."

"You're on my route. I'll get to you around ten-fifteen."

"That sounds right. Listen, ring the bell, we'll have a cup of coffee."

Annie stepped out of the post office into the bright sun, the long grass by the walk light green from the heavy rains. The answer to the riddle was simple and had nothing to do with her: Philip's clever older daughter was watching, and he had to lie low. She would see him after class and tell him she understood, just as he had expected her to understand. Such a thing was not of real importance.

During the morning it was as if weights had come off Annie's feet, so she could walk lightly in the spring air—she thought of Emily and her cartwheels. But through the early-afternoon class, which Philip taught with his usual vigor, giving her no sign, her confidence flagged. She got as far as the Union, afterward, walking with him and three other students, when uncertainty grabbed her and she made an excuse to run back across the grass and up the fire escape to the costume studio.

Ellen had quit at the semester; there was no risk of someone intruding on Annie as she buried herself to sob in the musty garments which hung in the back. The familiar smells of mothballs, dust, old cloth sobered her, and she pulled away from the dark folds to see what work she could immerse herself in. The sun through the skylight stung her swollen eyes. All the layouts for *Cyrano* were spread over the cutting table; the costume for the poet himself hung over the sewing machine, while tacked on the wall nearby was a Dutch portrait of Henry II, which she had copied for her design. She had wanted a different Cyrano—all the old drawings were of a kind of clown or dandy, dressed brightly in red and green. The portrait was in muted golds and rich browns with a touch of magenta braid, faded with age, decorating the jacket. It was painted in the Stuart era, and Rostand had written later on, but she liked its simplicity and grace better than the fussy Baroque style. She had finished the satin shirt, its lace collar falling soft on the shoulder; the coarse wool for the pants lay uncut on the table. She had stuck to real wool, even though it was expensive and hot. Now she was working on the jacket, in velvet, the vertical slashes on the sleeves edged in braid to accent the white satin that would show underneath. She had basted in the lining yesterday, and it had to be stitched. She pressed her palms to her closed eyes for a minute, to remove the sting; then, taking up the jacket, she stretched it carefully as she slid it under the foot of the machine. The sun warmed her back and lit up the clean tables, the neat piles of fabric, the swept corners, the starched dresses grouped by color and period, the rows of dyes over the sink, the masks staring grotesquely from behind the glass of their case. As Annie worked with quick precision in her hands, she let the pained thoughts knocking at her mind pass through, and not once, as the afternoon sped by, did she stop or even take note of their current.

It was close to 2:00 A.M. when Annie stumbled home from the studio, drugged with fatigue. At some point during the evening there had been a rehearsal for *Cat on a Hot Tin Roof;* late the next morning, as she struggled to consciousness, she dimly remembered cast members milling in the fitting room, needing tucks here and gathers there, a new bow tie for Clyde, who was naturally playing Brick. Mona had ripped her seam again, and she had been angry with Annie for finding a dress that only made her feel fat. But the students had drifted away and left the hollow continuity of hours, the low hum of the fluorescent lighting. Around midnight Annie had stood by the window and eaten a moldy orange she'd found in the thread box, and watched a lone student hurry home along the path under the eucalyptus. The citrus oil had stung the tips of her fingers where she had pricked them with pins, and the juice had quenched the dryness of her throat. She hadn't felt hungry until now, waking heavily, like a diver rising through dark water. Her stomach was a cavern.

She had slept through her first class. Pushing away the sheets, she had just planted her feet on the cool floor when there was a knock. She shrugged into her robe and went to answer, thinking that if it was Philip she didn't care, but instead she faced Didi Decker, smiling brightly through the screen door, a heavy blue postal sack weighing down her left shoulder. "Ding-dong," said Didi.

"Postman always rings twice. God, I forgot. Come on in. I'm a mess."

"You got your phone bill, some junk about panty hose, and a letter from your dad."

"You read it?"

"No, but the return address says Al Redfield, and the handwriting looks too old to be a brother's, and he calls you 'Miss.' "

"You're a regular sleuth. The P.O. should fire you."

"Return address is Taiwan. How come?"

"International software sales. My father's business. Coffee or tea?"

"Tea, please. Herb if you've got it." Didi set her heavy pack down on the desk. "Caffeine and acid make holes in my stomach. I bought bagels."

In the bright, cool kitchen, Annie felt puffy with sleep. As she heated water she combed her hair out with her fingers. "How's the route?"

"After three hours, still okay. Here's your letter. And a cinnamon-raisin."

Annie opened the envelope and scanned the short, slanting lines written on a postcard inside. "The usual," she said. "It's raining a lot and what do I want him to bring back. He hardly expounds philosophy, like some fathers." She tried to disguise her blush with an offhand grin and took a quick bite of the bagel. She *would* have to bring in Philip.

"Hey, don't get the wrong idea. He talks more about poker and bonsai. I never knew he was thinking all that stuff till I got to Berkeley and people told me about him." She took the mug of tea and followed Annie into the main room. "You like him a lot?"

"Your dad? Sure, I like him. He's given me a lot of help." And heartache, she thought, letting her coffee burn the roof of her mouth.

"Nice place." Didi had taken the green chair. "What're all the sketches?"

"They're mine. I do costumes."

"For fun?"

"For a living. Or I will, when I'm out of here."

"You're not going to grad school?"

"No way."

"Huh." Didi sipped the tea, her eyes hovering around Annie's face, not quite resting there, the only unsteady feature of her solid, wide-awake countenance. "My father'll be disappointed."

"I don't think so."

"Oh, he will. He thinks you're smart, he told me so at that party. Guess he doesn't know you're talented too." She rose and toured the room, as Philip had done, studying the sketches. "Caesar, Antony, Lady Macbeth. Hermione," she read, stopping. "Who's that?"

"Character in *A Winter's Tale*—Shakespeare, not performed much till recently. I worked on it in Ashland last summer."

"Ashland, Oregon?"

"They had this festival."

"And you designed for it?"

"Oh, God, no," Annie said around her roll. "They've got pros for that. I was just fiddling with ideas. They kept us peons busy putting together muslin mockups and dyeing things. All the costumes were built from scratch."

"Built?"

"Put together—designed and sewn."

"I used to sew," Didi said, going on to the other *Winter's Tale* sketches—Leontes, Perdita, Florizel. "But I gave it up—seemed too domestic, you know?"

No, Annie thought, Philip's daughter wouldn't do as a seamstress. "Come by the studio sometime," she said, a twist of vanity in her voice. "It's a little different from making aprons in Home Ec."

"I bet it is. I'd like to get involved in theater. I was in a play at Berkeley."

"Well, if you stop in, I'll put you to work. My assistant just quit."

"Then I'll come by. I want to be useful. I came home partly because I wasn't of use to anyone, up there."

"I guess we all feel like that sometimes." The bagel was making a cold, hard knot in Annie's stomach; she washed the last bite down with coffee. "You'd better get going," she said to Didi. "Your route."

"Neither rain nor snow nor gift of gab. I like the Hermione sketch best." Didi put down her mug and hoisted her bag. "I'll stop by again, okay? Just to see if you're home. If you've got time."

"Sure, just knock. Thanks for breakfast."

"I knew you'd like it." Didi's grin was almost coy. "See you!"

◇   ◇   ◇   ◇   ◇   ◇   ◇   ◇   ◇

Didi came by at the same time the next three days, stopping in for tea and staying just long enough to exchange a few questions. Annie forced herself to get out of bed and dressed before Didi appeared. Moving against what seemed a sea of inertia, she washed dishes and put papers away; she didn't want word of her torpor getting back to Philip.

"Did you do this?" Didi asked, standing in front of the one framed picture in the room, the light from the ceiling reflected in its glass.

"No. I can only draw clothes. My friend Mona got that for me in Mexico."

The painting was a watercolor of abstract golden fishes pouring from a net into a red boat, the rich blue of the sea covering the background as if the boat itself were under water. The fish seemed to stand on their heads and to balance on their tails, like acrobats. "It's perfect for you," Didi said.

And the next day, in the costume studio: "Who was that I passed on my way up here?"

"A woman named Mona."

"Oh, your friend."

"Well, she was. We used to play a lot of tennis together. There's been a kind of a . . . rift. She's wrapped up in her boyfriend. But she's in this production, so she needs a costume."

"Sounds awkward."

Annie nodded, bent over a layout.

"I bet you started out wanting to act, before you got into design."

Annie grinned. "I've never stepped onto a stage, and I never intend to."

"I told my father I'd seen your stuff, and it was good."

"What'd he say?"

"He laughed. Stuff like art makes him nervous."

The following day Annie rose in time to shower and make it to her early-morning class. Afterward she stood leaning against the kiosk at the corner he always rounded on his way to get coffee. "I think I deserve a piece of your time," she said as he made the turn. "For a talk."

Philip's eyes stirred toward her face. "You do."

They walked across the quad without speaking and stood in the shade of a eucalyptus, its long branches swaying slowly in the breeze. Annie shivered; out of the sun the air was cool.

It was only fair to have a talk; it was only decent. Night upon night she had framed what she would say to him—if he was leaving her because she had told Mona, she would confess that like a girl she needed a best friend. If it was something at home, something to do with Didi, she would persuade him to trust her, to embrace her now and then for five hurried minutes in some abandoned, hidden place, rather than shut her off out of fear.

Didi was at her door now, stopping by on her rounds with the mail. Later she might visit Annie's studio and break into the silence there, gabbling like a brook while Annie kept on with her work. *I push her away,* Annie thought, *as he does me.* She looked up at Philip, the spotty shade of the leaves moving over his face and neck, his shirt open at the collar. He was waiting, here, inches away, in the present. Her long, fidgeting sleep had left her red-eyed, and she knew she did not look pretty. Nothing she said would sound right. She had nothing to say to him.

But he spoke first, a relief in spite of the words she had known were coming: "Annie, I think we should stop seeing each other."

Now, that's impossible, she wanted to say, *we have to see each other until I can get my thesis done and graduate. You mean we should stop screwing each other.*

But no. Distant and civilized, she answered, "That's a bit of a switch. I'm the one who's supposed to have something to lose."

"Yes, that's true. And perhaps it would be better for you if we stopped."

Screwing each other. "Don't patronize me, Philip. I'm leaving here in June." When he made no answer, she went on, "I guess it's rumors. We're getting too obvious for you."

"No, no, that's not it. I don't think anyone actually knows. They suspect, but they're not sure."

It was not the others, then. Of course he would have said if it were. Mona and Didi were stick figures, phantoms of her own invention. She had to kick away her adolescent mourning and make a leap to where he stood alone, face to face with her. "Can you tell me why?" she asked softly.

"The truth is, I'm in a sort of emotional turmoil." He looked away and fumbled in his pocket for a cigarette.

"And you think it will be any better if we stop now."

"I don't know." With effort, he finally looked straight at her. His eyebrows had drawn up toward the middle, and the pupils of his eyes were like rocks. "I just don't know."

"Well." Pulling a long leaf off the tree, she took a deep breath, counted, and let it out. "You tell me when you do. I'll be around."

She couldn't understand; she set herself against understanding. She had wanted the affair to last until she left—no more than that. But she saw an end coming at her, black and faceless, before its time, as Philip walked away.

Didi was sitting on the lower step by the garage below Annie's apartment, her pack on the step behind her. *Oh, go away,* Annie thought, and then she thought, *oh please stay and hold me Philip.* "What's wrong with you?" Didi asked as she picked up her mail-bag and followed Annie upstairs. "You look exhausted."

"Yeah, well, I just had a confrontation."

"With a professor."

"No. With a friend."

"Your friend Mona?"

"No, no—someone completely different, you don't know them." *Them,* the perfect pronoun, sexless. "It's a long story."

"Do you want to be alone?"

"No, of course not. I'm okay." Annie pushed open the door to the dark room. The air inside hung stale. Opening the window, she sat on the edge of the bed, and the cool breeze flowed over her back and shoulders. Didi was in the kitchen already, heating water. Annie reached for a cigarette, found the pack empty, and crumpled it.

"You should quit anyway," said Didi from the doorway.

"I know."

Didi crossed the room and sat next to Annie on the bed. She reached out a hand and stroked Annie's hair, pushing the loose strands back from her face. "Is there anything I can do?" she asked.

"You can hold me."

Didi moved back on the bed, behind Annie. Gently she wrapped her arms around Annie's shoulders and, when Annie said nothing, began to rock her. Annie was surprised; but drowsily, as if in reverie, she dropped her head on Didi's breast and folded her hands around the girl's hips. When she felt Didi's lips on her hair she flushed, pulled away, and wiped her eyes. "I can't," she said.

"Can't what?"

"Can't—let you. It's silly, I'll be all right." *But touch me, touch me.*

Didi kissed Annie's forehead and brushed her cheeks like a nurse. "Well, then. Let's have a smile." Annie smiled obediently and kissed her in return, with a short, nervous giggle. The color had receded from her cheeks, and while the rush of blood left a small knot of pain in her head, she felt light and intoxicated. Didi sat cross-legged. "Should we talk about me? Will that help?"

"Sure. What about you."

"I met Mona last week. And I liked her. Well, sort of."

"I'm not surprised. She's a likable person."

"She said she loves you."

"How did you get that out of her?"

"I just did. I was jealous."

"Oh, come on."

"Really. Girls at Berkeley are so superficial. When they want a serious relationship, they turn to men and sex. It would never occur to them to care about another woman. You and Mona are lucky." The kettle whistled from the kitchen. "*You* stay here," Didi said. "I'll get it."

She stayed until noon, sitting apart from Annie on the bed, talking, and Annie sipped tea like a convalescent and let her go on. Annie missed Mona; she missed Philip. She could see him in Didi's face in the morning light that soaked the room like butter, and in a crazy way she wanted Didi to touch her again, to give her comfort.

Lying on the bed after Didi had gone, she remembered how Didi had leaned forward as she talked, earnest and coaxing, with no trace of craft. And yet there is craft, she thought. She doesn't have to speak so much of her father and of men. She doesn't have to fill in so many gaps. She wants me, wants to get her father out of me. I want her, want her father in her.

But she, Annie the liar, had given away nothing, had not missed a beat. Or had she? She thought of Didi's face, her young female Philip-face, and its very openness seemed a decoy. Oh, she needed a friend. She considered calling Mona. It had been weeks since she had found Mona backstage, hours after she had run from Annie's apartment, her wood clogs like hooves fading away down the pavement. She had been crouching in the stage wings, dressed in a black leotard and black jeans. "It was idiotic of me," she had whispered, watching the stage. "I should've guessed he'd be there. I'll return your key. Clyde and I don't use it anyhow."

"What, are you back with him?"

"Ssh, not so loud. Yes. I am. He looked like a coward, you know."

"Who?"

"Your Philip. The way he hid his face. I'm on now—we can talk later." She glanced at Annie, then away, and walked out into the lights.

Annie had known they would not talk later. She could not call Mona now. Even if she did, it would not help, because then she would only lie to Mona too.

Another week passed. An eminent and incomprehensible logician from Finland came to town for a series of evening lectures, and afterward Annie left the lecture hall alone, though she noticed that Keith Clarke, the junior member of the department, followed her partway. Keith had taken up spying seriously, skulking after both Annie and Philip, dropping by Philip's house to find him absent, then catching him later to ask, mincing and sly, where he'd been. Keith had his own crowd of students, shy, slight boys adept at probability theory, who had suspiciously started to pick up conversations with Annie. Keith himself caught her at odd moments of the day to gossip about Philip Decker's past and a girl named Linda—did she know that story? *It's all through with us!* she wanted to shout back at him.

After the last lecture there was a reception at Keith's house, arranged by Keith, with wine and cheese and witty conversation. Jack Wheelbright brought Ruth, a tall, large-boned coffee-skinned woman with a close-cropped natural, to show her off. Urban Whittaker arrived with whiskey and a psychology student, a sophomore, her mascara gluing her lashes together, who drew Annie into the kitchen.

"C'mon," she said, leaning close, "you can tell me all about it."

"About what?"

"About *Phil.*"

"Nothing to tell."

"You know, we followed you home on Halloween, another girl and I."

"What for?" So they had seen her, kicking him out.

"I think he hates me."

"He doesn't hate you."

"Maybe you and Phil and Urban and I could take a little trip somewhere, a vacation. Wouldn't that be *neat?*"

"Urban and Philip are both married, I think. Excuse me, I've got to get in on the discussion out here."

"Oh, yes, yes, of course. Phil's so sweet, don't you think? And so brilliant. He scares me. Doesn't he scare you?"

Annie moved out to the dining room. Jack was sitting by himself at the table, selecting corn chips from the basket to assemble in the shape of a star, while the others moved in and out of the room. "Come here and talk to me," he said. "You can't hear yourself think in the other room."

"Where's Ruth?"

"Flirting with the dean, getting Brownie points. They're threatening to close out her position at the Black Studies Center."

"I heard they might close out the whole Center."

Jack picked out a chip, stared at its curled edge, tossed it back. "That too. One trustee said she could stay and be his mistress. A taste for darkies."

"I don't believe you."

"You'll read all about it my book. Porno book." He twinkled his eyes at her. "Just a joke. Hey. Has Phil been talking to you?"

"About what?"

"About me—what they're trying to do to me."

"He did ask some questions about the class last term." Watching Jack for clues, Annie chose her words carefully. "He wanted an idea of how students had felt about it—he didn't say why."

"Did he grill you about the classes I canceled, or about the times I quit lecturing, when I—"

"When you started to shake?" Jack nodded. He had turned the star around; it was now a pentagon. "No, nothing like that. Why would he want to know about your classes?"

"He didn't tell you?"

"No—I just said he didn't."

"They want me to take a sick leave—Urban and Philip and the president. They think I'm too strung out to teach."

"Will you do it?"

"Hell, I don't know. If I thought it would prove something to them, I would. But they'd just be watching more closely when I came back."

"You don't think it would do you any good, then. For yourself, I mean. Wouldn't you like a break from all this?"

"There's nothing wrong with me. If I take a break, it'll be for my own reasons."

"To write your porno book."

"Exactly."

The subject was closed. Jack took a chip from the pentagon, snapped it in two, and ate it. He shaped the remaining four chips into a square. The psychology student moved past them into the living room, winking at Annie as she went by. "Quite a crowd here," Annie said. "I see people who walked out of the lecture."

"I'm surprised Phil's daughter didn't come—she said she would. You know Didi, don't you? I've seen you together."

"Sure. We're friends, sort of. I'm teaching her to sew."

"Bright girl, Didi," said Jack. "Very grown up."

"She seems close to her father."

"Oh, yes. I'd say they understand each other. You know about Linda."

"Doesn't everyone?"

"Well, so does Didi."

Annie stared at him. "How did she find out?"

"I told her."

From the next room, the hum of discussion had reached a grating pitch. "But why?" said Annie, suddenly queasy. She leaned back against the chair for support. "What good did that do?"

"Well, she asked me, sort of. You have to understand, Linda had made herself a friend of the family. Didi was only fifteen, and Linda took her out to movies and told her about sex and pretty much spilled the whole thing herself."

"Why?"

Jack shrugged. "She was proud of it, I guess. Wanted someone who cared about Phil to know."

"Where do you come in?"

"Well, I'd known Phil for years, and Didi since she was a little girl. And I knew *all* about Linda. I was the natural one for Didi to turn to." Jack was leaning across the table. His eyelids blinked rapidly, and he squeezed his thumb against his index finger. "She was very confused, of course. She couldn't really grasp why such a thing would happen. Subconsciously she felt guilt, as if she was lying to her mother whenever she said nothing. But I explained the causalities to her, and I think she understood. She's always been closer to him than to Joan anyway. More wine?"

"Thanks—I'll get it."

Annie backed away from Jack to refill her glass. Sidling out to the living room, she picked an unobtrusive spot on the edge of the couch and watched the exchange of fire around the cozy room. Philip ignored her. He actually cared about things like the Principle of the Mean. He listened awhile and then piped up with, "What I think you want to say is something like the following:. . ." There followed some erudite remark—he always spoke in colons when he wanted clarity. Keith had put on a Bach record and was standing in the corner with a group of male students engaged in a heated argument on fugue. One of the students, Dave Prince, disengaged himself from the corner group and circumnavigated the room until he reached Annie's perch. "You look like you need some air," he said.

"I'm sure I do."

They moved out onto the porch, where a Santa Ana wind blew warm and dry over the chapparal. The air was always dry in this part of the country, even now, during the rainy season. Standing with Dave, Annie thought of Michigan, where the sticky summer heat had pressed down on the air throughout the night, while in the winter the damp would enter and stiffen the sleeper's limbs to ice.

Dave passed her a joint. "I'm sick of this dilletante chit chat," he said. "Don't you want to go out for a snack or something?"

"No, thanks."

"To my place, then."

"No." She was sitting on the rail. He leaned against it, the porch light gleaming on the long, straight bangs that fell over his eyebrows. He was from Detroit too, a prep-school boy. They used to go skating together. "I'm trying to grasp the ineffable," she said.

"Okay, if you're sure." He moved his hand onto her leg. As it rested there, she thought how he could hold her, could take her in his awkward, muscled arms and stroke her hair. For a moment she wanted to go with him to his room and have him make clumsy love to her, coming too soon, then take her out for ice cream or pizza. But she put her hand over his and said she was sure, and he left.

She went in. Realizing she was drunk, she drank more. The circle in the living room had broken into little clusters, and she found Philip in the pantry, putting away the cheese. His mild, indulgent smile made her want to irritate him. "Take me home," she said. "I'm smashed, and it's too far to walk anyhow."

"No problem. Wait while I get my jacket." Annie stood out on the porch, letting the wind revive her. It had begun to rain again, with slow, fat drops gradually darkening the pavement. Philip returned with an umbrella, which he opened and held over Annie as they hurried out to his car. She glanced back to see Keith watching them from the doorway.

Out of sight of Keith's house Philip pulled Annie's head to his shoulder. For the length of the ride, neither of them spoke. When he pulled to the curb Annie said, "You can just let me out. It's my period anyway."

"I've got the umbrella. I'll walk you up."

They embraced like old lovers, easy and sad. He unbent her arms and kissed the inside of each elbow, then her legs and the inside of each knee, and her resistance broke away like mica. Her flesh, full in its season, flowed over him as she moved on top. She arched and cried out, then sank, her breasts soft against his granite chest. He traced her spine with a finger. Later they lay on their backs on the bed, the rain outside incessantly knocking, while he told her about the old house where he'd grown up in Texas. His room, he said, had been a makeshift one at the back, and he used to go to sleep with the rain crashing down onto the metal roof.

The downpour increased, the wind driving it straight against the windows. Philip stayed a long time, waiting for it to let up, and Annie almost thought to hold him there, in the warm room that was like a dry, dark egg. But at last he dressed, the old ritual, switching the light on like a knife. She followed him out the door and down the steps—if the eggshell had shattered, it didn't matter whether she was in or out. And it seemed so absurd to leave like that, in the middle of the night, in the shivering rain.

Chapter 3

INFERIOR

CONJUNCTION

◇

"If Epiphenomenalism is not attractive to Decker, it is clear the Identity Theory is," Philip read. "In the last section of his paper he says it is simply a fact that by random mutation higher animals evolved brain states 'which are of the sort that are identical to mental states.' What sort of brain states are these? Decker does not say, except to state that these are of an 'unknown character and configuration.' "

"Jesus Christ," Philip said aloud.

"What's that?" Joan called from the kitchen.

"Oh, I'm just annoyed. *Thought* sent me the draft of Panacci's response to my response to his paper, and I've got to write a rejoinder."

"Does it ever stop?"

"Yes. I get the last word. But I have little left to say. I've pointed out every fallacy in his argument, I've demonstrated the viable alternatives, I've admitted the no-man's-land of ignorance in which we're both living. We don't *know* that much about brain processes, or their evolution, but that's simply not the point of the debate."

"What is?" Joan appeared at the door, dressed for bed.

"That the identity theory is perfectly consistent with, and even supports, the theory of natural selection. Panacci distorts the whole notion of survival of the fittest to claim that without sufficient evolutionary *cause* for isomorphism, there can be no evolutionary *consequences* of it. I've met Panacci—he's a nice guy, a bright guy. But he's bullheaded, and he will ignore even objections he knows to be valid in order to restate his point eloquently and preferably with sarcasm. You going to be up for a while?"

"Yes. I've got my maps spread all over the kitchen, so I guess I shouldn't quit now."

Joan turned away, and Philip bent back over his desk. "Okay, Panacci," he said. He wrote: *Evolutionary explanations are a type of functional explanation.* Simple English—no more principles of systematic isomorphism or nomological connections. He had crossed out whole phrases in the draft before him and replaced them with symbols, and as he wrote he made diagrams, to highlight the points which were obscured by long clauses and qualifications. . . . *That is, the occurrence or existence of an item or process is explained by reference to the function it performs for some system. For example, someone might functionally explain the presence of his typewriter in a room by noting that he used it for writing letters.* Philip turned to his typing table and examined the machine. At the back on the left side the words "Moose Jaw, Wisc." were engraved in the metal. What the hell, he thought. *Now, suppose that his type-*

writer is identical with the millionth machine manufactured in Moose Jaw, Wisconsin. Thus, in many contexts, the fact that he uses his typewriter for writing letters also explains the presence in that room of the millionth machine manufactured in Moose Jaw. The fact that he uses his typewriter for writing letters does not, however—nor need it— explain the fact that his typewriter is identical with the millionth machine manufactured in Moose Jaw.

"If you can't understand this, Panacci," he said to himself, "you know nothing about typewriters, not to mention biology."

Philip wrote until his hand grew cramped. He lit cigarettes and smoked them halfway, then left them in the tray to burn out before lighting another. When he stopped, he found he had grown tired from all the thinking, as if from physical exercise. It made him hungry too. He got up from his chair, unlatched the window and opened a crack at the top to let in air without creating a draft. He heard the rustle of paper in the kitchen; Joan was still up.

She was bent over a map of the Topatopa Condor Refuge which she had taken down from the wall. Places where she had spotted birds were marked in different colors, according to the year, and dated by month. She was drawing up a chart, using the places and dates as references.

"How does the stalking go?" Philip asked as he entered the room.

"I don't know. It still looks pretty chancy."

"Well, it's all you've got, isn't it?"

She sighed. "I suppose. Still, I wish they'd given us more for research. We'll use up the funds following the slim leads we've got, and then when we've learned from our mistakes how to capture a bird, there won't be any money."

The grant had come through, and Joan had funds for a spring and summer search for a male condor. If mating was successful within a year, the Recovery Team could try more extensive controlled breeding. If the attempts to capture or to mate failed, the federal grant would not be extended; the project would shut down.

"How does Lucius feel about it?"

"Oh, he's euphoric. He's sure we can get a fine specimen—'a stud,' he said—and that we'll find one within a few months. It's the right season. But I'm awfully depressed. I guess I should be glad to be able to do something, but what if we catch a nesting female? Or what if they won't mate?"

"You do all you can, don't you? Some species go extinct, others survive. Modern civilization to one side, it's a natural process. According to Panacci, the fact of that process should stand in the way of all my theories, but it is a fact, nonetheless. Want a hot brandy?"

"Sure, it'll help me sleep." She began to fold up the graphs. The lines in her face spelled tension; she bit her lower lip as she tacked the map back up on the wall.

"You're working too hard, Joan."

"No, I'm not. This thing just upsets me, that's all."

"Will you be able to forget about it, in England?" He mixed the brandy with the hot water and put it back on the fire for a moment. She liked it really hot.

"I hope so. Remember the avocets?"

"The ones in the marsh? Sure." Early one morning they had approached a swamp in the Cotswolds, where the shingle had spread over its banks and left an apron of stone and sand in the midst of brackish pools and reedy flats. As they had drawn close, a dozen of the speckled birds, with their upturned bills and long blue legs, had lifted off together and resettled in the low mist a hundred yards off. The species had been considered extinct for sixty years—it was the closest you could come, Joan had said, to seeing a flock of pteradactyls. "Maybe the condor'll pull the same trick."

"It'll be nice to be back there," Joan said when the table was clear and they were both sitting with their brandy glasses. "Spend some time with the girls."

"And each other."

She smiled. "You're good to say that."

"I mean it."

"I know."

What did she know? *A strange heart—I can't account for it myself,* he wanted to tell her. *Forgive me your pain, I didn't want it.* "It's funny," she was saying. "I really love those buzzards. It sounds corny, but I've spent so much time with them. When I go down to San Diego to study Topa, I feel as if I carry their smell on me, that he—she, I mean—knows that I've been with her kind, even though I never get within a hundred yards of them. And they're so ugly. They've always been ugly, but somehow they seem uglier now that there are so few left. It's as though they would have become beautiful if they could have survived. When I get close enough to see the expression on one of their faces through the binoculars, sometimes they look tormented to me. I know that's absurd, but they do—they look tormented."

"You should have been a nurse, Joan."

"And you should have been a doctor." They laughed softly. It was a small joke between them, that they had met in a medical library and now found themselves in these fields, so far apart. At first the teaching and writing had just been a job, a vocation—a choice. Now he could feel his mind at work like a spider around him, spinning out skeins of thought and wrapping him up.

And there she sat, his wife, trying to save a dying species. She was unhappy, and not just because of the birds. Her breasts drooped slightly in the nightgown; her whole body seemed to droop just a little, like a plant in need of water.

And he? He was happy—there lay his guilt. Discontent but happy, even excited. He supposed that was what he wanted to tell her, though he never did. Between them hung his lies to her, and in the quiet room they were almost audible. Yet she remained the one with the mystery. He patted her hand.

"You'll be up late?" she said.

"I imagine so." Wasn't it better, still, that he was happy? He could give it back to her later, tenfold.

"Well, I'm for bed. Lucius is coming by at six. We're going up Cobblestone Mountain." After she had rinsed her glass and set it on the rack, Joan kissed him lightly on the head. It was a mother's kiss, a dry benediction, and he didn't like it. "Good night, dear," she said.

"Night."

Annie stood outside Philip's house, looking in. With the shield of night, she could see everything in the lit house, while if they looked out they would only see themselves in the window. She stood in the tall bushes next to the house, where no one approaching could see her. At first, not trusting her own invisibility, she had been afraid to come this close. But they looked straight at her now and then, and there was no sign of recognition—they really couldn't see past the pane, not even he could.

It was sometime after midnight; that was when she'd left the apartment. She didn't know how long she had been standing here. She knew this was irrational—when she finally went to bed on nights like this, it was with the decision that she really was losing control and she would see a shrink in the morning. In the morning she shrugged the feeling off. But in the middle of the night, when she couldn't concentrate anymore and there was no one to drop in on, the obsession stole over her again. What was he doing? Saying? Who was with him? Could he, at this moment, be turning away from her once more? She asked herself what he looked like—to her horror she found she couldn't remember. The shape of his chest was there, the smell of the skin, but not the face. Then she took off her robe and put on jeans and soft sneakers and a dark sweater and walked rapidly over to his house, passing it and then returning, carefully, in case she had been seen. The streets were empty, blank under their lights, and the few houses that were lit shone like cats' eyes. She went a different way each time. Once she had been just approaching when a car went by and turned into Philip's driveway. It was he, alone. Where had he been? Had he seen her, just now? She crept along the fence, crouched down, and watched him get out and go into the house.

He hadn't even glanced in her direction, and she had been strangely disappointed.

The house was large for the town. The easterners who built here had brought their clapboard with them; they couldn't adjust to adobe. The wide front porch faced a broad lawn with only one magnolia, but the side was full of bushes and two oaks stood at the back, behind the garden. The property was surrounded by a redwood fence—picket but not painted white, not in the West— with three gates for entrance that clicked sharply as you un- latched them. Annie never did, but swung her legs over the fence where the magnolia shielded her from the house, then bent down quickly and waited to see if anything stirred, if there was an eye caught by her movement. Nothing blinked in the house. Gener- ally three rooms were lit: the kitchen, Philip's study, and one bedroom upstairs—Didi's probably. Sometimes the upstairs room was dark, and once the light had gone off, startling Annie while she watched from the back. She had pictured Didi in the dark, stretching out in the bed, her thick hair slowly matting against the pillow, her limbs sinking against the sheet.

From the magnolia she would walk along the fence, bordered on the other side by a neighbor's thorny hedge which caught at her clothes. At first when she reached the oak she had stopped— from there she could see Philip in the study at his huge oak desk, bent over a blotter white with scattered paper. He leaned his forehead on his hand, which rubbed it occasionally as if to un- cramp a thought. He wore his half-glasses, but when he stopped writing he took them off, ran his hands over his face, and looked up at the ceiling. When he wasn't at the desk he was in the armchair in the corner reading or writing something different, letters maybe. Sometimes student papers were scattered around. From the oak tree Annie could see only his legs and hands when he was reading, but when she drew closer she had a full view of him. Sometimes he was dressed; more often he wore a robe, brown plaid flannel edged in blue. He'd never wear it for her. His wife had given it to him, probably—how could he accept a gift like that from her? Nonsense, how could he refuse?

Joan was almost always asleep. Once, though, she had appeared at the door and seemed to be asking Philip to come to
bed. She too had been in a robe—from him?—and nightgown,
her hair crumpled around her face. At least not in rollers, Annie
thought. She looked almost pretty, diminutive and fragile in the
doorway. Out of the severe clothes and sharp glasses she wore to
work in the mountains, she seemed young for a woman in her
forties, a young mother, just beginning to give herself over.

Now all the lights but the one in the study were out. Philip was
putting books back into his massive bookshelf—soon, Annie
knew, he would go upstairs to join them, leaving only the night
lamp in the living room burning. The living room was the only
place she'd been in the house, when Philip had hosted a reception
the year before; she remembered noticing the original paintings
on the wall, huge canvases. Now he turned back to the desk, facing
her. The window was open a crack at the top, over her head, and
she could imagine the warm air of the house slipping out. "See
me," she whispered. She was tired of being outside the window,
watching in this obsessed way. What if he did see her, how would
she explain? She tapped lightly on the window, then drew her
hand back as if it had been stung, and hoped he hadn't heard.

He had. He came over to the glass and peered out, then
lowered the top pane. "Hi!" he said.

"Hi." He wasn't angry with her for coming. His voice sounded
just like his voice, the familiar trace of a drawl; somehow that
surprised her. Hers, she thought, squeaked.

"What are you doing here?"

"I don't know, exactly. I guess I just wanted to see you—I
missed you. I'll go before I wake anyone up."

"No, wait, I'll come out. Go around to the back porch."

Obediently she went around the corner of the house, feeling
that after all her caution they were making a horrible racket. He
switched on the porch light, came out, and sat beside her. "It's
good to see you," he said before she had a chance to apologize.
He really did look glad to see her—proud, almost, that he had
lured her so far.

"I really ought to go away. I feel silly for coming."

"Let's take a walk," he said. They went out by the driveway, the gate clicking loudly, their feet crunching in the gravel. "I've been working on that essay on evolution for *Thought*," he said. "I told you about it. It's kept me up late."

"I've been working on that thesis on perception for Decker. I haven't told you, but he's a tough outfit to please. It always keeps me up late."

They walked around the block. "Want to go for a drive?" he asked.

"But your family—"

"I'm a grownup. I can go where I want."

When he started the car Annie thought the roar would make every light in the house, or in the block, jump on. But nothing happened; they were all asleep. He drove up to the mountains, black against the stars that poured into the sky as they climbed higher. Annie opened her window and leaned out. The air was cold, and the wind pulled at her face. Turning into an overlook, Philip shut off the engine. Below, light littered the valley—how could she have thought it dark enough to hide her, down there? Maybe they had all woken up and switched on lights, and when they drove back Joan would be waiting.

"Pretty, isn't it?" said Philip.

"Mm. From here."

"I bet this is where teenagers come to neck."

"That's hard to do, with bucket seats."

"We'll get out." He pulled a blanket out of the trunk and spread it over a level place on the scrub. Annie leaned back—the wind died here, close to the ground. The weeks of rain were scarcely noticeable at this altitude; the chaparral smelled dusty and bitter. Behind them, the face of the mountain reared up like a storm. He leaned over her, and his breath as he spoke seemed the only thing moist and warm in the world. "I'm happy you came tonight," he said.

"Are you really happy?"

"Really."

They remained until the stars had shifted their positions a near-visible degree. The road downhill went faster than the climb. "Don't you wish we could just keep going?" Annie said when they reached the main intersection at the foot. Their way led back to Newhall, the fork headed east—Las Vegas, Denver, New York.

"Wishing like that's a bad habit. You shouldn't get into it."

"That means you do."

"I won't say that, it'd support your vice." He pulled into the parking lot next to Annie's place but kept the motor running. "I have to get back," he said.

"I know, I know."

"I wish—I wish a lot of things. There's no sense talking about them. You know what they are anyway."

"I guess I do." She couldn't think of his wishes, but she looked with a settling calm at his eyes, and saw only herself there.

◇   ◇   ◇   ◇   ◇   ◇   ◇   ◇   ◇

Jack nabbed Philip outside the philosophy building. "You haven't got a class now," he said. "Get some coffee from the office for a change and come on. I'm giving my first Heidegger lecture of the term."

"You know what I think of Heidegger, Jack."

"I know what a brilliant lecturer I am. Something you and Urban have forgotten."

"We haven't—"

"I've been a little off, I know. But I'm on today. When I'm done with those kids in there, all the women'll be in love with me, and half the men, including the straight ones. I want to strut my stuff for you. Come on."

He grinned like a kid in the bright sunshine, and Philip realized he had forgotten how handsome Jack was. His enthusiasm lit up his fresh, unlined face; it was impossible not to want to gratify him. "What are you on?" Phillip asked.

"Nothing, Well, okay, a little benzedrine. But it's prescription. I'm riding on the ideas, really. You'll be sorry if you don't come."

"Class observation."

"That's exactly right. And we're late!" Jack bounded up the steps ahead of Philip, his sport coat flapping.

Reluctantly but not without curiosity, Philip took his coffee into Jack's classroom and found a place at the back. It had been over two years since he had heard Jack lecture. The students were mostly freshmen, with a few nonmajors who had thought "Philosophy of Mind" would give them lofty ideas. When Jack walked into the room and stood before the lectern with only a small piece of chalk in his hand, there was a quick rustle of paper while they pulled out notebooks and pens. Standing stock-still except for the thumb and forefinger that rolled the chalk, Jack eyed the room. Then he began to speak.

"At some time or other," he said, "each of us here has probably had the experience of being acutely aware of himself—or herself. I don't mean being aware of any of our personal characteristics or our peculiar features or the situation we find ourselves in. We simply become aware of the fact that we exist."

He stopped to let that sink in. He looked excited about it; they, in turn, looked excited, as if Jack were going to tell them the secret of their existence. That was why they had taken his course.

"It's uncanny, isn't it?" he went on, and they nodded. "And it's often accompanied by feelings—of despair, of elation. But the experience is not particularly mystical, is it? In the experience one is simply aware of oneself as existing. At the same time one confronts what is obvious but usually eludes us: that one has no choice but to be oneself and to make of oneself what one can, given the limitations that being oneself imposes. Say you're in a wheelchair. Well, at that moment you're not aware of the wheelchair or your missing leg, but in being aware of yourself, the wheelchair and the missing leg are givens—Heidegger calls this the 'grasping in which *Dasein's* nature is ascertained,' but let's not get caught up in his words just yet. I want to deny mystical status to this

experience because the experiencer doesn't gain any special knowledge through it. No insight into the reasons, if any, for his having
been brought into being. No glimpse of the fate that's going to
befall him—or her. Therein lies Heidegger's whole problem."

Eyes shifted, papers rustled. The students' hands wrote as fast
as they were able, taking down what Jack was saying. He spoke
clearly, with only the slightest inflection; his face wore an un-
wavering slight smile, as if there were just a possibility that all
these ideas were a joke. But he thought the way the young people
he faced were thinking, and they clutched at the sentences that
came from his mouth and that they would not read in the pon-
derous books he had assigned. He spoke as one who understood,
and this, too, Philip had forgotten.

"If you ask me what the color of a particular ashtray is," Jack
went on, "I know how to go about answering. Color-talk is
complex, but we know its rules. Some people"—a covert glance
at Philip—"think that color-talk is philosophy. Some people
think talking about what is pain, and is the world out there real
or fake, is philosophy. They debate through millions of pages
over naming things. That's not Heidegger. Or me. We know the
rules of color-talk, but if you ask me what the *being* of that
ashtray is, I'm at a loss to know even what to look for. It's more
embarrassing even than talking about love."

Philip thought of Annie's yellow pencil, the slings and arrows
of outrageous fortune. It was just like Jack to bring up love in a
classroom.

But he was going on: "I might wonder whether I heard the
question correctly. In contrast to color-talk, the rules of being-
talk are anything but straightforward. One is tempted to call talk
about being"—he moved the piece of chalk across the blackboard—"*n-o-n-s-e-n-s-e.*"

After an hour, Jack stopped abruptly and asked for questions.
Philip scanned the room. He could almost hear the minds racing,
and Jack had been right: they were all in love with him. He had
lifted the veil, he had cured their blindness. With his level voice
like a magnet and his nonsense on the blackboard.

I haven't his gift, and I haven't his beauty, Philip thought. And I am famous, and still sane, while his career and his soul have burned to ashes inside him.

Yet for a moment Philip would have traded places with Jack, whose life would always be governed by his needs and his inner fire, his quest for being. Jack had failed to win Annie Redfield— but for that same moment, Philip thought she had chosen wrong. What woman wouldn't want to bring back the flame that had been Jack? To humanize it?

Well, there were plenty. They clustered around Jack at the end of the class, their earnest faces aglow, but the magician they were looking to impress had vanished: Jack stood, hollow-eyed, answering questions in monosyllables. When he saw Philip rise, he turned abruptly from his students and followed him from the room.

"What did you think?"

"You were fantastic. It was an intoxicating experience."

"So why don't you tell Urban to cut this crap about a medical leave? I couldn't deliver a lecture like that if I were about to go over the edge."

"Do two things for me, Jack." Philip stopped in the corridor, knowing he was right to be stern in spite of Jack's genius, but also knowing he spoke from jealousy more than from wisdom. "Go back to those kids now. Answer their questions. Then do it again tomorrow without the speed."

"That's it. Do it right. Like the rat that learns the maze, he hasn't got it right till he does it every time. Well, this rat has its eye on you too, Phil. When it's your turn to snap, it'll know way ahead."

He turned and walked stiffly back toward the hall from which students were streaming to their next classes. Some tried to catch him for a moment more—Philip heard echoes of "Mr. Wheelbright, Mr. Wheelbright"—but Jack only stopped and stood like a statue in the corridor. The students looked up at him first with anticipation, then ruefully; without wasting much time they turned back to their friends and ran giggling down the stairs.

◇   ◇   ◇   ◇   ◇   ◇   ◇   ◇   ◇

Cyrano was in performance. Next came *Cat on a Hot Tin Roof,* and then the season would be finished. The only costume left for Annie to worry about was the dress that Mona had brought to her apartment weeks before, which she would wear as Maggie. It still didn't fit across the bust; Mona kept splitting the side seam in rehearsal, and George had ordered her to lose weight. Living on orange juice and celery, Mona let loose her irritation every time they had a fitting and the dress was still too small.

But with everything else completed, the students who had worked at the studio were all wrapped up in final projects, and Annie could repossess the room as her own. She threw away scraps too small even for trimming and sent the rest of the year's costumes to the laundry. From the trunk of unused fabric she was choosing a few large pieces to keep for herself—left behind, they would only grow stiff with age.

The theater department had not moved to replace Annie. "Why don't you stay?" Ellen had asked. "I'm sure you could get a raise. They'd have to take you on as a professional."

"But I'd never learn anything new. I'm waiting to hear from a place in New York, then I'll know what to do."

"What place?"

"American Academy. A woman I worked with at Ashland is there—she told me they're taking on designers."

It had been over a month since Annie had applied to the academy, and still she had heard nothing. She had told no one, even Philip, about her plan, though she waited impatiently for the mail that Didi brought each morning. If the academy didn't take her, she was afraid she *would* stay on at Newhall. It would be too easy.

Sorting through the unused fabric, she found buried deep in the trunk a large piece of pure cotton velour, its taupe pile the color of a rain cloud at sunset, which was to have made a king's robe but hadn't stood up under the lights. She stood before the mirror and draped it around her so that the material fell in rich folds to the floor. She would give Philip a farewell present, she decided. Something to finalize things. The robe she had seen him wearing in his study had been an old flannel, sagging at the elbows, the narrow collar faded. He would have a new one, soft against his skin, loose in the arms, trimmed at the neck in burgundy.

He would have to explain a new robe to Joan. But that was his problem. Annie was the gift-giver, the departing one.

She had to stay at the theater during performances, in case anything ripped on stage and to collect costumes at the end of the evening. She spent the time in the studio, laying out the thick fabric, marking it to a pattern, cutting, pinning. She scarcely heard the actors' voices or the applause, and twice she forgot they were there until the cast broke in to hand over their costumes.

The robe would be magnificent. Having washed the dust from the velour, she steamed it lightly on the reverse so as not to crush the nap. She bought two yards of burgundy satin for the wide collar and cuffs and the edging of the pockets. A thinly padded interfacing could make a sandwich between satin and velour; she would quilt the collar and cuffs like a Chinese smoking jacket. After looking through all the books, she had drafted the pattern herself—the robe had to be luxurious but not dandified. After constructing so many false clothes, barely sturdy enough to last a few nights on stage, she found it difficult to pay attention to details, the inside workings, matched notches and trimmed curves. She stitched French seams throughout, first joining sections with the rough edges outside, then lapping the cloth back and enclosing the seam in a narrow lip.

She worked herself into the robe, into Philip. She knew how each fold of the cut cloth would lie against his skin, wrapping over his shoulders and cinched to his waist, falling loosely over his buttocks and legs. When she lay against Philip in the late afternoons, she imagined herself the finished robe as she grazed his chest with her lips, wrapped her arm across his ribs, let the light from outside reflect off her face onto his. The closer the robe came to perfection and the more she disappeared into it, the more perfectly it embodied everything she thought she could ever give to Philip. It was a gift which in the end wore his stamp and not her own. When she had finished at the studio for the night, she went home weak with an effort that went beyond the late hour and the work.

She had little else to do. The thesis was complete. After he had had it for two weeks, Philip finally brought the manuscript along to lunch. "This is excellent work, you know," he said.

"I should think you'd disagree with a lot of it."

"I do. You reach many wrong conclusions. You've still got fortune in there with her slings and arrows. But there are occasional flashes of understanding and originality. I think Jack should read it—he'd be crazy about it."

She rolled her eyes.

"No, really," Philip went on. "I heard him lecture this morning. He's still got that old charisma, when he wants it, and he'd have a lot to say about phenomenology and the creative process."

"Haven't *you* got any criticisms?"

"Not really. I've made a few notes on a loose leaf at the back. Here." He handed her the manuscript, bound in black vinyl to be shelved in the library, and took up his sandwich. The outdoor café was noisy and crowded at noon on this, the first really hot day of spring. She glanced at his notes. They were sketchy and hesitant. Disappointed, she pulled out the sheet and handed the thesis back.

"Think you'll go on with this stuff?" he asked.

"Not a chance."

"Smart girl." He smiled at her across the table, and she thought of the gift she was making for him. The hours she had spent writing the thesis telescoped into a few dull, distant moments. After all, his lack of response and the discontent that had pricked her were over a few pages of abstract theory, nothing more.

The robe filled her inner senses. She smiled back at him and bent over her salad, crisp and sweet. A relieving stir of wind lifted the tablecloth and Philip's hair as the sun poured down over them.

◊ ◊ ◊ ◊ ◊ ◊ ◊ ◊ ◊

Polyurethaned wood was the keynote of Jack Wheelbright's apartment. He had used it for door frames, shutters, cabinets. Its dark, sticky-looking finish gave the place the impression of having just been painted, and Philip was always surprised at there being no smell of fresh paint, but only of the incense Jack burned in the corner to cover the stale odor of unwashed clothes and dishes.

Jack had set up the card table in the center of the main room and positioned trays of nuts and a cooler of beer within arm's reach so no one had to get up. It had been over a year since they had played poker at Jack's place, mostly because Jack never delivered on his IOUs and no one wanted to give him the impression that hospitality would be accepted in exchange. But they had run out of other places. Joan was working at home every night, and Harriet claimed to be redecorating. The fourth member of the group, Stefan, was out on the East Coast looking for a new job—his appointment in biology had not been renewed. So they had wound up at Jack's, with Didi filling in for Stefan. They had to limit the games to five-card stud and blackjack for Didi's sake.

"Hit me," Didi said.

"You're sure, now," said Philip, who was dealing.

"Don't give her tips," said Jack. Didi had sixteen showing.

"I said hit me."

Philip flipped the card slowly onto Didi's pile. It was a two.

"I'll fold," said Urban.

"Me too," Jack echoed.

"Well, I'll raise you ten." Philip pushed a blue chip to the center of the sagging table.

"I'll see that. And raise five," his daughter said. They had to be careful pushing chips around, because the table was too small for cards and drinks and chips, while the shag rug underneath was too unsteady for the drinks; as it was, accumulated chips gathered around each player's chair leg. Now Jack leaned forward to straighten out the bets—he liked to have each color of chip in a neat pile in the center of the table, like building blocks—and he bumped the corner with Urban's fresh beer on it.

"Holy Jesus Mary mother of God," said Urban as the foam sputtered down his pants leg onto the rug. The bottle spun round to the table center and drenched Philip's score sheet before he righted it.

"I can't believe it. I just cannot believe it. Out of the way, everybody," Jack cried as he raced to the kitchen and came scurrying back with a torn bath towel. "I just had this fucking rug cleaned."

"Well, you *are* becoming an old lady, aren't you, Jack?" Didi said as they lifted chips and cards for him to wipe under.

"You try paying for rug cleaning on a teacher's salary, little Miss Coed." Jack was on his hands and knees on the floor, almost tearing at the speckled green shag with the towel.

"Damp it, don't wipe it. Here." Didi took the towel from him and stepped carefully on it to soak up the beer.

Philip and Urban watched impassively, exchanging glances. Behind his poker face, Urban's countenance said, *You see? Everything he touches turns to lead.* Urban had trimmed his beard sharply down so that his round pockmarked cheeks hung over the pointed bit of stubble at the end of his chin.

"Well, the smell will linger," Jack was saying.

"Who'll notice with the incense?" Didi retorted. "Place stinks like an opium den already. Get loose, willya?"

"Listen how they learn her to talk at Berkeley," said Philip, and winked at his daughter.

"Get loose." Jack sank into a chair. "I'll try that." His long, elegant legs stretched out to where his ankles crossed below the neat cuff of trousers. "Loose means knocking off when you feel like it. Right? Okay, so the game's over. Everybody go home."

"Don't be an ass, Jack," said Urban. "I'm thirty bucks off, I have to recoup."

"We didn't even finish the hand. Look." Didi picked her cards out of the bowl of nuts and turned the last one over. "Twenty-one."

"Thought you were bluffing," said Philip. "Take the pot. That's three times your allowance."

"Don't I know it!"

"No, really. I want you all to pack up and go home." Jack yawned loudly, covering his mouth with the beery towel. "I'm ahead, and I currently have plans for the money. And Ruth is coming over in a little while to discuss the plans. But the three of you can wrap up a hand or two, I guess. I'll just watch."

"Do we get to hear about the plans, Jack? Or is this just a punishment for staining your rug?" Philip asked, drawing up his chair and shuffling the cards.

Jack didn't answer, letting silence fall as Urban dealt for five-card stud. In the pause Philip considered how he had tried to do his duty by Urban and the department, these last weeks. He had been to another of Jack's classes—an hour of meandering drivel, this time—and had cornered Ruth outside the Black Studies Center. Suspecting hypoglycemia, he had persuaded Jack to see a doctor about physiological causes of his mood swings. He had even pumped Annie for student gossip. But Annie held him at bay, while Jack, who used to put him through soliloquies of anxiety, had kept mum about the checkup and his moods. "You're sure you never slept with him?" Philip had asked Annie the day before.

"What, you think I'd forget?"

"He knows about us. He's hostile."

"He's jealous. I can't help that. It's as much jealousy of me as of you."

"Jack's not gay!"

"He's had a crush on you. You're turning him over to the wolves."

"I'm trying to get him to seek medical help."

"He doesn't want medical help. He wants love."

"Well, he won't get it from me. Or from you!" He'd pointed a finger at her.

"I'm not a professor-fucker, Philip." She had jerked her head up and sniffed in pride. He hadn't been able to get out the words to tell her he was only teasing.

"Let's make a gamble on the game," Jack said now. "Urban, if you win, I'll take this leave you're proposing in order to screw my ass to the wall. Phil, you win and no leave."

"What if I win?" said Didi. "I'm on a streak."

"Ah. If the little lady wins, she has my hand in marriage." He stretched out his hand to her, palm upward.

"Ugh," she said. "I won't play, then."

"She's underage," Philip said. "I'd never give my permission."

"I never thought you saw age as a barrier to lust, friend," said Jack, leaning over the table. He had had too many beers, especially for a hypoglycemic. His breath came warm onto Philip's face.

"Pick up your cards," Urban interjected. He lit his pipe so the smoke rose between Philip and Jack. Pursing her lips and smiling like a Mona Lisa, Didi began to sort her hand. Jack pushed himself back from the table, leaving it to wobble, and they all steadied their drinks. Philip glanced sideways at his daughter, but her eyes were glued to the cards.

The game went quickly. Urban and Didi each took three cards, Philip only one. In the discomfiture of Jack's dare, they laid extravagant bets, Philip and Didi finally seeing Urban at sixty bucks. Jack paced the room, scooping up crumbs and peanuts, emptying ashtrays; he rattled the vacuum cleaner in the closet once, but didn't bring it out. The players showed their hands: Urban had been bluffing with a pair of twos, Didi had three nines, and Philip a full house. "*Damn* it," said Urban, with more vehemence than sixty dollars justified.

"I don't get any of this," Didi said, turning her eyes from Urban to her father.

"Aha!" Jack approached the table. "That's it, then. Just as I predicted. Gentlemen, to my newfound freedom."

"You've got it wrong, Jack," said Urban resignedly. "Phil's won. You stay at Newhall."

"Uh-uh. Phil won, so no *leave*. Leave meaning temporary absence. I'm following Didi's example—I'm dropping out."

"I don't *get* it," Didi moaned.

"Don't you, Miss Coed?" said Jack. "It's simple, really. Department can't be down more than two suckers. Urban here is on his way to Shangri-la. I have just now, this moment, announced I'm quitting."

"What if Urban or I'd won?"

"If Urban had won I'd be taking a leave and *then* quitting. If you'd won we'd be taking an extended honeymoon."

"Not on your life."

"But in any case I'm departing Newhall. It's May already, so they'll never replace me by September. And your daddy had plans for a trip to Mother England. Which he'll have to scrap. But he doesn't mind, really, no matter what he tells the wife and kids. He rigged the whole thing, see, so he could stay right here in *honey*town and—"

"Hey, I left the ivory tower because the *students* were screwy." Didi said. "I don't want my escape to sanity ruined by you eggheads and your problems." She spoke quickly, staring Jack down; Philip had pressed his thumb and forefinger to the bridge of his nose, as if he had a sudden headache, and considered punching Jack before another word escaped his sculpted mouth. But Didi went on, "You guys can stay here and lay the weirdest kind of bets you want. I'm trading in my chips. I only promised to stay till ten anyway. I told Mona I'd meet her in the set room."

"Who's Mona?" said Philip, lifting his head. That name was familiar.

"A new friend." Didi had pushed back her chair and risen to get her jacket. "I'm getting to know some people in the theater here. She needs help painting flats."

"So you're getting to know the Newhall girls again, are you, Didi?" said Jack. He had taken her chair at the card table and poured himself a fresh beer.

"Yeah, Jack, I am. Only we're all college women now, you know? All in the same boat. 'Bye, Daddy." She bent to kiss his cheek and he squeezed her hand, still trying to place that name, Mona. "Don't wait up for me." Her lips were cool against his cheek.

"Mysterious creature, that girl," said Jack as she closed the door behind her. "Now, Phil, old man, you want to hear about this prize you won?"

And like an old crony, he took a pull at his beer and told them all about it.

◇   ◇   ◇   ◇   ◇   ◇   ◇   ◇   ◇

Later, Annie wondered if she had meant to put Mona and Didi together. So little happened innocently or by chance. That night when, her weight supported by Philip's hands cupping her breasts, she had taken possession of him again, she had gained a slight—a minuscule—advantage over him or anyone else in deciding the future. Yet that advantage frightened her, because it might actually give her what she coveted, and once she had it she would risk a greater loss than if fate had denied her desire. She thought of Mona's "mentor condition," and saw it as a state into which everyone fell in some way, because everyone needed external boundaries on what could happen to them. There was always an excuse to cordon oneself off. And somehow Annie must have known that, in the long chain of events, if Didi and Mona forged a link they would eventually fence her out of the life that called out to her, and so allow her to think always that it might have been different.

While she waited for Mona to come for her last costume fitting, Annie opened the windows of the studio and let the night breeze float in. May had arrived, quick and subtle, like a woman in a silk dress whishing into a room, and the air was soft and scented with hibiscus. As she leaned out over the sill, she remembered the first time, a few weeks back, that she had seen Didi and Mona together. Outside it had been raining hard, probably the last rain of the season, and she had been listening to its drumming and looking out at the fat drops that splatted into the gutter and then rivered down the pipe and onto the soggy ground. The water on the closed window had blurred everything outside, as if the natural colors were paint that was running together into a uniform gray. By contrast the hanging costumes in the studio had seemed startlingly separate and bright. Outside, a striped umbrella that Annie recognized as Mona's had appeared on the walk below, and cupping her hands against the glass, Annie had been able to tell the other figure underneath was Didi. They had been leaning together, and she had thought she heard Didi's laugh.

It had hurt. It had actually hurt in her heart, as if a valve were constricting. I'm jealous, she had thought then. As the performance had drawn near, Annie had begun to notice Didi more often with Mona and Clyde, too. Didi had enrolled, late and at Mona's suggestion, in a Newhall set-design workshop, and they would all eat ice cream at the Union, their clothes splotched from painting screens.

Then just last week Mona had stopped by the studio, full of the old breezy cynicism that had charmed Annie almost two years before. But of course, Annie had thought, she's got a new best friend. "With this strip tucked into the side the dress'll fit fine," Annie had said.

"And none of my other clothes do, and I'm sick to death of cottage cheese." Mona had inspected herself in the mirror. "It's still tight around my boobs. I don't know how you're supposed to reduce there—that's the way I'm *built*."

"Does it hurt?"

"My stomach's the only thing that hurts. Are you still sleeping with Philip Decker? If Didi keeps living at home she's bound to find out."

Annie had been putting pins into the hem. "How? No one else knows."

"Don't be naive." Mona had started to pull her leotard back on. "Things with Clyde are awful," she said. Lighting a Tiparillo, she had stood by the door while Annie tacked up the hem. "He doesn't sleep, he's flunking his classes. He blames it all on me, but he's never home. When he is, it's because he wants quiet or something to eat. I keep thinking he's sleeping out on me, but that's not it. He'd be no good at hiding it." Her voice had had the lilting monotone of a practiced speech, a test of Annie's patience. Didi had no doubt heard all this already.

"It's more like he's sleeping with himself," Mona had gone on. "He's consumed with himself. I'm sick of it. He never asks how things are going for me, he just takes and takes like a child, It's terrible, but I can't break away. You know? I've been telling myself for so long that I've had so many relationships and that I've got to make one work and that I'll regret it if I end it like I did with Bruce."

Annie hadn't looked up until Mona stopped abruptly and gathered up her purse and books. "But I guess you don't want to hear all this," Mona had said in an altered voice, her hand on the doorknob. "You don't really give a fuck about me and Clyde."

Then Annie had turned from the sewing table to face her. "No," she had said evenly, knowing that if this was a test, she had failed it. "I used to, but I guess I just can't anymore." She had let the taffeta dress slide to the floor as Mona banged the door shut behind her.

There was just this one fitting left, tonight, and then she would never see Mona again, never have to speak to her again. It was past twelve already; Mona had promised to stop in after her evening class. Annie turned from the window. She couldn't wait all night.

As she flicked off the lights in the closet and main room, she heard steps on the fire escape. She opened the door, and light from the lamp fell on Mona's blanched face. "What's the matter?" Annie asked.

"Is Didi here?"

"No. I haven't seen her all day. I thought you were coming to try on the dress."

"Could she be at your apartment?"

"I haven't been there for hours." She came down the metal

steps to where Mona was standing, out of breath. "What have you done?" Annie asked, though with the words out she already knew.

"I've told her. About you." Mona's hair was wildly disheveled, her hands clenched; one of her shirt buttons hung loose. "But that's not all. Come on, we have to look at your place."

Annie locked the door and followed her down the clanging steps. The hibiscus scent seemed already a mask on the true night. They ran across to Annie's apartment, but the steps there were empty. "Didi!" Mona whispered anyway, as if she were calling a cat from hiding. "Didi, are you here?" Annie opened the door and Mona followed her inside, turning on lights in the kitchen and bathroom as if Didi might be waiting there in the dark.

"Have you checked at her house?"

"She wouldn't have gone there."

"Well, what did she say, when she left?"

"She said—" Mona stopped her searching and came to sit on the edge of the green chair. "She said she should have gone to bed with you. That way she'd have found out your affair and stopped it, all at once."

"Gone to bed? With me? Didi?"

"Instead of with me." Mona pulled at her tangled hair. "That's where state secrets are given out, you know. In bed."

In bed. Annie groped for the wall behind her and slid down to crouch against it. "What are you telling me?"

"That you don't understand anything, Annie."

"Don't say that!"

"Well, what do you want me to say? That we're all confused?"

"What's confusion got to do with it? You made . . . I mean you—went to bed—with Didi. And then she ran off, and God knows what she's going to do. Is that right?"

"I made love to Didi. First we have to admit that. I kissed her, I went down on her, I made her come."

"You don't have to give me the details."

"Yes, I do."

"Why?"

"Because I did it with her instead of with you. Because I did it with her on *account* of you. And she did it with me because— well, because she's that way, for one thing, but also because she wanted answers. She told me she'd always envied her father's women. Not because she wanted to make love to her father but because she was sure he told them things, in bed, that he would never tell *her*."

"What about you?"

"What about me?"

"Are you that way?"

"I don't think so." Mona kept working on her hair, combing out the knots with her fingers. "But I was tonight. And I have thought about you, that way."

"I thought," Annie almost whispered, "about Didi. Like that. Once. But it was only because she reminded me of Philip."

"You see? We are all confused."

Annie pressed her hands to her temples. "Tell me what happened as she was leaving," she said, groping for practicality. "How come you're so worried about her?"

"Well, we were just lying there—you know—"

Naked on the bed, little pockets of perspiration under arms and breasts. One pair of breasts dropping away from the other as if newly created, like cells splitting.

"—and she was telling me how her father used to take her out to the desert, just her, alone. Then she said that thing about wishing she'd gone to bed with you—"

Didi stroking Annie's hair back from her forehead, brushing her cheeks like a nurse, with that bent smile, her father's twin.

"—and suddenly she got up and grabbed her clothes and dashed from the room. She said, 'I'll show them'; I remember her saying that. And she ran out. I lay there a couple of minutes, trying to think what I'd done. To make myself believe it. Then I panicked. I thought she'd come to see you."

Mona had given up untangling her hair and sat primly with her knees pressed together, hands folded on her lap. She was thinner, from the dieting, especially around her face and neck; her chin looked small and pointed. Her sitting there, so proper in her dishevelment, like a schoolgirl—she looked younger, with the weight loss—made Annie feel old and calm, even as her heart raced with the knowledge that everything, everything now, had changed.

"We'd better find out if she's home," she said. "I'll call Philip."

"What if her mother answers?"

Annie thought for a moment. "I'll ask for Philip. Because if Didi's not there, I'll want to talk to him—and if she *is*, I'll want to know what she said to him. I'm a student, I'm allowed to phone my adviser."

"It's way past midnight."

"So I'm a rude student. Christ, Mona. Didn't you think there'd be consequences?"

Mona bit her lip again and said nothing. Annie lit a cigarette, tossed her the pack, and went to the kitchen to call Philip.

◇ ◇ ◇ ◇ ◇ ◇ ◇ ◇ ◇

It was 4:00 A.M. when Philip started up the road that led to the desert. He had taken Joan's Volkswagen, which had more gas. He liked it better for mountain driving too; it held the curves in third gear without his touching the brakes, and it would roll down the far side of Cobblestone Mountain like a metal pebble. The muffler needed replacing and gave out a fluttering roar.

He had delayed, after Annie's phone call, only because of the sheer foolishness of it. Didi had never been a flighty girl. When she had learned about his affair with Linda, she had said she would tell Joan about the next one. So now Annie's friend had spilled the beans—he had expected Didi to come home as soon as her anger hit the boiling point and to blast him with his infidelity.

Joan had been asleep when the call came. She had already dozed off when he'd gotten in from the poker game, and when he'd asked her then about Didi, she'd mumbled that she thought

Didi was in her room, but she didn't know, she might have gone out again.

After talking to Annie he had sat up in the dark living room, in the chair where he'd already been pondering Jack's bizarre announcement. Drinking scotch, he awaited Didi's return from whatever parking lot she was occupying in her beat-up Toyota, letting her filial wrath build up steam. But she did not come, and still she did not come. At 3:30 he had called Annie back and tried to learn everything Didi had said, to give him a clue, and when Annie told him she had mentioned the desert, he knew he had hit on it. What had led him, then, to tiptoe upstairs and check Emily's room, he did not know. But there in the glow of the night-light were the empty white sheets, the bare pillow. Didi had moved quickly and silently, stealing her sister away, while he had stayed out with the philosophy boys. He did not wake Joan, but ran to her car and headed out along the road that Didi had known he would follow.

He rounded the mountain and pulled onto the gravel turnout. The gibbous moon, invisible from the west side of the ridge, had just risen over the next range, and he could barely make out the shadows of the manzanita hedging the road. The plain below was moonlit, but he only perceived a cobbled surface representing the low-lying scrubs and clumps of cacti. He did not get out, but shut the headlights and peered over the dashboard, trying to see something moving below.

He had always taken Didi to the choicest spots for the flowers, luxuriant corners off the main road on the way to the glider field. They would drive to a few and then find a picnic place sheltered from the wind and driving sand. When they had finished talking about bees and pollen, cycles and seasons, she would tell him about the latest outrage her teacher had committed at school or about what she would do when she was twenty-four. ("No *way* I'll be married," he remembered her saying matter-of-factly, "but I'm sure I'll have my share of lovers.") He, in turn, had warmed up and started divulging things she had no way of comprehending—theories and hypotheses, complaints about colleagues, school politics. He had taught her to be wary of the world, a lesson perhaps he had no right to teach.

He started up the car again and drove down the winding slope to the plain. Here the road straightened out, a taut black string pulling at the car. The speedometer crept up to eighty, which felt like a hundred. No lights swept the asphalt but his own, which soon picked out an incongruous stop sign looming ahead. He slowed and turned right, onto the dirt road that led to the glider airport. Bumping along this same road after lunch, they used to send up clouds of dust which settled on the flowering cactus by the roadside.

The sport had not gotten any more popular, and the road was as treacherous as ever. When Philip banged his head hard after a bump, he pulled over and began walking. The moon was higher now, the upper side as if smashed, deforming the face. He could see some yellowish blooms on the ground, but he did not recognize them. It was full season for desert flowers, and she hadn't asked him to take her out here. He had never lost her so completely before, certainly not with Linda.

Confusedly thinking back, he saw he had been as blind then as now. Didi had padded behind Linda like a puppy for weeks, going with her to the Mall, getting Linda to sneak her into campus movies. Linda had thought it hilarious, and Philip remembered flaring with anger when she had sent Didi home one night sick on tequila. Then one afternoon Didi had sat alone in her room for hours, the shades drawn, crying without making a sound. But she had been at that age when young girls are supposed to be morose and preoccupied with themselves, and Joan had thought she was upset because she was overweight and wore braces, and because she and a friend at school had just vowed to give up their passion for horses. But when Didi came out of the room, what he had read in her tear-swollen face lay far removed from teenage anxiety. *Why didn't you tell me?* it said; and then she answered her own question, staring him down: *Because you didn't have the balls.*

He had reached the dirt strip now. No sign of her Toyota, but they had to be here somewhere. The prop planes stood in a row, nosing up at the moon; he knew how, inside the hangar on his right, the gliders' more delicate wings overlapped in the small space. No wind blew, but the desert air was close to freezing, and he had brought no sweater. "Didi!" he cried once. "Emily!" Then, as much to keep warm as to look for them, he began to jog down the smooth strip. The yard posts flashed by as they had while the glider's tow plane was accelerating for takeoff. He used to turn and wink at Didi as the glider left the ground, and as soon as they were high enough he would wave his gloved hand to signal the prop to leave them there, suspended in the still air. After gliding on a current of tepid air, they would hit an updraft; he would fold his hands behind his head and cry out, "She's yours!" and Didi would grab her wheel and spin it wildly, certain the plane would plummet as soon as she took command. Instead they jerked upward and turned a full circle before she lost the draft and the plane began to drift again. Finally they settled back to ground, turned in their goggles and helmets, and headed for the Cattleman, where she got a Seven-up and he a martini.

He would never take Emily gliding—too dangerous. How he had changed. He was panting now, the saliva thick in his mouth. He began to doubt his hunch. What would Didi do with Emily, once she got her here, a cold, tired, and terrified six-year-old? Suddenly he stopped short, the cold air caught in his lungs. The cry shot through the clear air—Emily, screaming, down at the end of the airstrip. His legs churned under him.

"Hush, baby, hush," he said as he reached the Toyota and crouched to hold her. Barefoot, in her bathrobe, Emily was cold as ice. The screams bolted from her throat even as he pulled off his shirt and wrapped it around her, as he stroked her hair and kissed her face. "Where's your sister?" he asked, and she pointed.

Didi lay behind a clump of grass a few yards away. Philip told Emily to stay and hush; her screams were quieting to sobs. As he ran to Didi he heard her moaning. He bent over her and lifted her head from the rough ground.

"Hey, Daddy-O," she said weakly.

"Where are you hurt?"

"Looky there." She pointed at her feet. "Ol' rattler got me. Wondered when you'd show up."

The left ankle, he saw in the moonlight, was swollen to the size of a baseball, and the swelling continued up the calf almost to the knee. "How long ago did this happen?" he asked, but she didn't answer. He pulled off her shoe and sock, then bent over the purple incisor marks, just above the Achilles tendon. They had swollen closed.

"C'mon, Emily, let's sit in the car," he said as he ran back. He swooped her up and sat her in the driver's seat, then rummaged in Didi's glove compartment until he found a jackknife.

Slicing neatly through the wound, he let the blood flow out and then put his lips to it and sucked. The poison had a sour, acrid taste, but there was not much of it—the rest was pumping through her bloodstream.

"Can you talk, Didi?" he asked.

"Ungh," she replied. Her lips were white. He pulled off his belt and wrapped it above the knee. As he jerked it tight, a rush of blood came from the snakebite, and Didi gasped and fainted. Her skin was fiery hot. He gathered her in his arms and stumbled back to the car.

"Is she dead?" Emily asked as he laid Didi down on the back seat.

"No, honey, no. She's hurt. Scoot over now, let Daddy drive."

"Can we go home now?"

For an answer he pulled her close as he switched on the ignition and spun the car around, the cold dust billowing behind them.

"I know about you and Annie Redfield," Didi said as soon as she opened her eyes.

"Ssh. You still have to rest."

"I know, that's all. And I'm telling Mother. You haven't, have you?"

"It didn't seem the right time. With Emily half-frozen and you half-dead."

"Thought so. Coward." She shut her eyes again and fell immediately back asleep.

The hospital room was spotless, bright with the midday sun. Philip had not been home since they arrived here at dawn. Joan had left three hours before, to take Emily home to bed, and she had not returned. They had talked little; Joan was waiting for him to explain all this. He paced the room for the hundredth time, stopping again to study the framed square of lace hanging in the corner. One edge had already grown frayed by the time someone had framed it, and he wondered idly how long the rest would have lasted.

They had praised Philip's tourniquet but removed it instantly and shot Didi full of antivenom. The doctor admitted it was too late to do much; with her fever hitting a hundred and four, there was nothing left but to wait for it to come down. Only an hour ago Philip had learned she would not lose the leg.

At six that evening Didi woke again. "Hey," she said, and Philip jerked his head up from his chest.

"Hey."

She sat up and yawned. "Man, I slept." She started to stretch and noticed the needle taped to her right wrist. "Can't we get rid of this thing?"

"Not till we're sure you won't peg out without it."

"Where's Emily?"

"Home. She's fine. Shaken up."

"Mom been here?"

"Off and on."

"But you haven't even gone home yet, have you?"

"Nope." He rubbed the stubble on his chin. "You're built like an ox, you know that?"

"Why? Should I be dead?"

"You should be crippled."

She leaned down to feel her leg with her left hand. The bandage covered her ankle and foot, and the rest of the calf was swollen to twice its normal size.

"You really haven't told Mom?" He shook his head. "What'll you do?"

"I don't know." He had gotten up to raise the blind on the window; the evening sky was cloudless, with an insidious layer of brown smog oozing over the horizon defined by the slanting light. Now he turned the visitor's chair around and straddled it, resting his arms on the back, facing her. "What were *you* doing?"

"I don't know." The fever had heightened her skin color.

"What did you *think* you were doing?"

"I don't . . . well, there's no way around it." She took a deep breath and touched the place where the needle went into her hand. "I was going to made this . . . sacrifice. To teach you a lesson."

"And just what were you going to sacrifice?"

She looked at him, her eyes deer-shy and fever-bright. "I wouldn't have. I already knew that by the time I was out of town. The idea's absurd. It just started because . . . well, there aren't very many ways of hurting you. Then I just kept going—driving, I mean. I'd forgotten the other thing. When I got there I told Emily to stay in the car. I was just going to walk out a ways, look at the place again, then head back. Then I stubbed my toe on a rock and stepped on the snake." She paused, then bitterly: "I love Emily more than you do."

"I doubt that." He watched her flinch and thought, punishing her, how glad he was to have her alive. "What did you want to teach me?"

"To see. Or maybe just to look." She reached down her leg again; he could see her hand feeling the swelling, under the sheet.

"Do you want to try some therapy?"

"No. Do you?"

"I'm never going to be perfect, Didi. I wouldn't have had kids if I thought I had to be perfect for them."

"Well, I don't need therapy. I just need to think." She shut her eyes and leaned back against the broad white pillow. Pale and pouchy, her face looked older than nineteen. "Why don't you take your Annie and go off somewhere?" she said, her eyes still closed. "Give it your best shot. As they say."

"You're suggesting I leave your mother?" She shrugged. "Leave all of you?"

"Mom's not exactly thriving in your relationship, you know. You might be doing her a favor. You could come back, I think. I mean, she'd probably take you back."

"But there's a lot involved. She—"

"Annie."

"Yes. Annie." He made himself say the name. "Annie's just your—well, she's a much younger woman. I've thought about it."

"You may not have much more thinking to do, after I talk to Mother. Unless you just want to give her up. And the others."

He eyed her sharply. "It's not like the others."

"Well, how should I know?"

Reaching across the chair back, he took the fingers of her free hand in his own and stroked them, one by one. He sensed dimly that there was more he did not know, more than the name of the person who had told Didi the truth, more than a fantasy of revenge by fratricide: why Didi had come home in the first place, what she was seeking for herself. "We have to forgive each other," he started to say to her, but he noticed that her fingers had gone slack and, looking up, saw she had dropped off to sleep again.

Philip had made certain decisions once, before he met Annie, when other women had merged for him into an abstract compulsion, a chink in the everyday world through which he occasionally thought he saw some new and dangerous light. He had determined not to hurt his family, Didi and Joan and Emily, and not to risk his work. Not to lose balance, and not to cause pain.

Was Joan in pain? He lay awake, a handful of days later, and heard her moving below in the kitchen. She was not giving out hints—no chances to redeem himself or to escape with a fixed measure of guilt.

Even her first reaction had given nothing away. He had waited—he found it was almost always better to wait—until Didi had returned from the hospital. There was always a chance that Didi would say nothing other than that she had gotten stoned and decided it would be a gas to show Emily the desert at night. Whatever punishment Joan meted out, Philip would have made up for. Beyond that slim possibility, he had prepared himself for a confrontation with Joan, alone, in which she reported what Didi had divulged to her and he denied everything. He had not thought that Didi would call him to witness her pronouncement. But her first night home, after Emily was in bed, she had put her head into his study and said, "Dad, I want you to come out here a minute."

Joan had already been sitting on the couch, her coffee balanced on her knees. She had watched him enter, followed by Didi, with no more than the restrained nervousness with which she faced any new situation—tension was ever her guide and her shield.

"Just a sec, Didi," he had said, hurrying past Joan, "I could use a cup of coffee." He let the kitchen door swing behind him. It was a stall for time, but as he heated water he found himself as ignorant and as expectant as Joan; he had no idea how Didi would go about this. After all, they were members of a family—intimate, long acquainted. Revelations were foreign to them. He made a cup of instant, stirred in milk, and stood in front of the refrigerator for a blank moment, then took a deep breath and strode back into the room. The two women sat facing each other, saying nothing, attendant on him. Didi's ankle was still heavily swathed; she wore loose pants over the swollen leg, and had propped her crutch against the bookcase.

"Okay, Didi, you've called this meeting to order," he said, taking his place next to Joan. "Why don't you give an opening address."

"You want me to tell her? You don't want to do it yourself?"

"I want you to say whatever you have to say." It was a small gamble, that maybe she wouldn't, but the odds were bad.

"Mother," Didi began, pursing her lips in disdain at Philip, "you have every right to know why I went off the other night with Emily. It was crazy. And I bet you haven't asked about it because you think maybe *I* was crazy." Philip glanced sideways; Joan had raised an eyebrow, but did not answer. "I *was* crazy," Didi went on, "because I can't stand to see what Daddy does anymore. You think he's this great husband maybe. Well, he sees other women. He's got one now."

Joan was looking straight ahead at Didi. "Why are you telling me this, dear?" she asked at Didi's triumphant pause.

"Well, mine was not the most reasonable reaction to the discovery. I'm telling you because it's your problem. I'm tired of going crazy over it. She's *young*, you know."

"No, I don't." Joan was wonderfully calm. "I hadn't known anything about it."

"Well, she is. It makes me sick. But I think maybe you're in love with her," she said, turning to Philip, "and you ought to stop playing hiding games."

All the denials stuck in Philip's throat. Joan's hand was next to his on the couch; he moved to take it but stopped short. "Her name is Annie Redfield," Didi went on. "She's a student, naturally. Freckles, small bones, nice clothes, not much of a figure. She sneaks over here at night sometimes—he's been sneaking over there since last fall. They meet twice a week, usually in the afternoon—you notice how late he is picking up Emily?"

"Didi, look at me," Joan commanded. "You've gone to a lot of trouble to find this out about your father, and to tell us both so. Now. What do you expect me to do about it?"

"Make *him* do something." Frustration scored Didi's face, and her clenched hands pressed against her thighs. "He's sleeping with her! He screws *around* on you. Holy God, can you people actually live out your lives together with this shit? I can't." She turned to Philip and added, "Annie can't."

She had done enough. He had to stop playing the spectator. Quietly, with what he hoped was authority, he said, "You'd better go now, Didi."

"Yes, dear, please leave us alone," added Joan, and Didi, speechless or pretending speechlessness, her face confounded with anger, pushed herself up from her chair. Reaching her crutch, she hobbled noisily from the room. They heard her jangle keys, open the front door, and after a minute start her car, racing the motor. Philip rose to close the door, then returned to the same place on the couch, next to Joan.

Lying awake, Philip recalled how peaceful the house had been at that moment, the calm after a storm. It was their home, they were at ease in it. Philip had put down his coffee and pulled Joan into the hollow of his arm. She fit snugly, neatly. "She's in a bad way," Joan said.

"I know. It's been coming."

"I wish I could help, but I've always missed with her. We can't hold a conversation at this point—I've no idea how to begin. She's your kid, really, even more than Emily is. I wonder why she came home from school."

"To finish growing up, I have a feeling. She's out to hurt me, not you."

They had sat there, weighing their losses. "I'm sorry about this," he said.

"Don't give me any explanations. I couldn't be interested. Didi seems to think you'll be leaving us."

"I wasn't planning on it. Not for her." Another lie, but one he could redeem: "Not unless you want me to."

"I think I do." She had not changed her position on the couch. With her back curved against the cushion, her small face and half-open mouth had tilted up at him. "Or I will. I haven't had time to think about it. I really did not know. But I've always wanted to make you as happy as you've been, these last months. That much I've managed to notice. She must love you better than I do."

"But not as much."

"No, not as much. But generosity can be learned. Passion's a gift."

"Which can be lost."

"No." She had sat up, pulling away from him. "No, but it might not matter in the end."

She hadn't yet told him what she'd do if he came back, or what she'd do if he didn't. "Oh, but you expect too much," she had said just today—impishly, even. "You want my permission and my promise to stay, at the same time." Last night he had tried, foolishly, to make love to her. They had wrestled in the heat, the sweat on them stinging, the way they had that summer before Emily's birth when they had strived to ignore Joan's thickening belly. But when he looked at her face there was hatred, not just for him but for what he was attempting. He had stopped and they had lain there; he blew on her chest to cool it down.

Now the bed was half empty, and cool. Would he come back to it, like this? Joan would wait, he knew, until she thought him asleep before coming up to the room; and indeed he would feign sleep to make it easier on her. After he left, he wondered, would she sleep in the center? He turned and tried to imagine Annie's slender form between him and the windows on the bed's far side. But all he saw was Joan's face from the night before, her moist cheek turned away, wishing he would give up.

◇   ◇   ◇   ◇   ◇   ◇   ◇   ◇   ◇

Annie didn't hear Mona enter the studio because she was sitting with her back to the door, hunched over the long table, hemming the robe. She made small stitches, catching each one within the loop of the next. "Who's it for?" Mona asked.

Her voice startled Annie, like a rap to the back of her neck, and she jumped up. "Oh, hi," she said, adjusting the cloth. "You scared me. I didn't think anyone else was in the building."

"I came back to find you. Who's the costume for?"

"It's not a costume. It's a robe for Philip. He needed one. It's a surprise."

"Hm." Mona came around the table and lifted a lapel. "Beautiful. Must've been a lot of work. I don't know where you find the time."

"Here and there, waiting out performances."

"I came to talk to you, before we both leave this place," Mona said. Sitting on the edge of the table, she lit a plain white filter cigarette and tapped her heel against the table leg. "I'm nervous, though."

Annie laid the robe over the sewing machine and sat down. "So am I." She was; she could feel her skin getting moist at the same time that it itched, slightly, all over. She had nothing to say to Mona. She had only questions and no courage for asking them. What had Mona been to her, after all? Not a friend so much as a force—a definition that no longer fit, a challenge she had finally declined. She had once imagined that Mona had found her, like a treasure. Now she understood that Mona had tried to invent her and failed, and like a half-finished model, she didn't know how to behave.

Mona smiled. "This is ridiculous. I really just came to tell you I'm sorry. We shouldn't be so tense."

"Sorry about what?"

"Not about Didi, if that's what you mean. She knew about you and her father already. She just wanted confirmation, and someone to share the blame, I guess. No, I'm just sorry about everything."

Annie had risen and unlocked the cabinet behind the cutting table. "Want some wine?"

"Is that what you keep in there?"

"For a rainy day," Annie replied, taking out a half-empty bottle and two dusty glasses.

Mona filled her glass and went to the open window where the moon, just past full, looked in. "Loving women," she said slowly, as if tasting the words instead of the wine. "It wasn't very sexual, for me. For Didi, yes. But I'd just . . . missed that, with men.

Being tender—no, exploring. It hasn't been the men's fault. I liked it, being with my own kind. It could happen to me again."

"You used each other," said Annie.

"Yes. But we got past that, just a little ways."

Annie joined her at the window. "Full moons are almost always my periods," said Mona.

"And this one?"

"Nope. I think I'm pregnant again."

"Mona! You can't be."

"Why not? Everyone knows the cap doesn't work."

"Clyde?"

Mona nodded. "I'm not telling him, though. I'll go in for a test in a couple of weeks, and if it's positive I'll get rid of it without saying anything to him."

"He'll notice."

"No, he won't. We're not together anymore."

"Sounds like something I've heard."

"I think I mean it this time. I'm going back East alone, I'll have the operation there. I wish I could keep it, though."

"Why?"

"Just because I feel great, right now. My body loves this condition. But later I'd hate myself. I'm no mother. And I don't want Clyde's baby."

Mona's voice was rich and balanced, like an older woman's. When she stopped speaking, the silence fell heavy. Annie poured them each another glass.

"I was apologizing," Mona said.

"You don't have to. There's a lot I don't understand, though."

"You mean like why did Mona turn her back on you when you took up with a married man?"

"I counted on you."

"No, you didn't. You made it through."

"There were times—"

"Okay." Mona held up a hand to acquiesce. "I was jealous. And, therefore, I disapproved."

"Jealous? Of me?"

Mona shrugged. "Of something I'd lost myself."

"Couldn't you get over that?"

"No."

Annie sat staring at the rim of her wineglass, as if she saw all her rage at Mona spread over its surface.

Mona spoke, finally: "You don't know what you do to people, do you, Annie?"

"I don't guess anyone does."

"But with you . . . it starts as a kind of passive seduction. You make people think they're safe when they're with you, and you make them think they're perfect. It's hard to resist."

"I don't mean to."

"Maybe you intend more than you realize." Mona finished her wine and refilled the glass. "With me, though, you have a problem. As soon as I feel safe, I look to acquire power. I start to run the show. It's better for you, in the long run, that I left you alone with your Philip. I'd have stopped you from going to him. You'd have hated me."

Annie said nothing.

"I've wondered about our love for each other sometimes," Mona went on. Her voice was softer, the jealousy absent. "I've felt more for you, in a certain way, than I have for any man—and more than I did for Didi, God knows—and yet we'd always sacrifice each other, if it came to that, for a man."

Annie nodded to make her go on. "I used to think maybe someday we'd live together," Mona said. "In a house, somewhere outside the city. Our men would come and go. Maybe we'd have babies, and care for them together. When men tore us apart inside, we'd heal each other. We'd let the outside world in now and then—it'd be intense and exciting. Then we'd close it out and make our lives all quiet exploration. We wouldn't be melancholy, the way we always are. We'd be happy. You see what you do? That's the sort of life you make me think of."

"You're ahead of me, Mona. I'm not ready for that life. Especially not the babies part."

Mona laughed sharply. "Nor am I. Obviously."

"I want to tell you to wait for me." Annie spoke as from an echo chamber, bereft of her honest voice. "I've loved you too, sometime back. But I've been isolated."

It was better, she thought, before we knew each other so well. That had been at the beginning, when they could each pretend they possessed an enchantment. They could work the spell on men—why not on each other? But there was no magic, nothing precious. That was the disappointment of knowledge: you found the ordinary. Mona's power, Mona's dreams, didn't matter. She was flat and transparent as a pane of glass, a window or a mirror, but as Annie groped for something more to say, she thought, I see nothing in her. Not myself, not the workings of her heart. "It's odd," she finally said, "that we should be exactly alike and utterly different at once. It's something Didi picked out, going to you." Her words came out on tiptoe, not quite light enough—giving, as she paused, little telltale creaks.

"We'll have to write, after we leave," Mona said, suddenly brightening. "Sometimes it's easier that way. I'll be in the East—"

"I don't know where I'll be."

"Maybe we'll get together, though."

"I'll be with Philip. Or maybe in New York. The Academy accepted me."

"I heard, I thought it was marvelous. Aren't you going?"

"I don't know. Things are confused now. I have to see."

"Of course you do. But if you are there—or if you wanted to visit—you could come to Philadelphia. My parents have a tennis court."

"I'm out of practice."

"You'd pick it up again. And then maybe we could talk. We need time, away from this place, alone, just to talk to each other. We have so much to express, don't you think?—to explore."

Annie nodded, out of habit.

Mona left, and Annie went home to cook herself supper. But instead of mixing eggs for an omelet, she took Philip's pint of gin from the ice box and drained it. She drank slowly, standing by the sink and looking around the room between sips. Then she went to the bathroom and retched. Very little came up. The bitter taste filled her mouth and nostrils, and blood rushed to her head so that she was dizzy when she stood up. She wished she could vomit more—that she could bring up all the cigarette smoke and wine, and the nasty thing inside her that charmed so destructively, that ate into everything.

"I'll tell you about the house we'd live in," she said silently to Mona. "Your side would always be light, while mine was always dark. Sometimes you'd come open the shades on my side, but they'd always close up again. Men would come to the house, but mostly they'd see you, dressed in black leotards, or red skirts, and your body would be amber color, like the sun. They'd want to bathe in the sun; they'd want to make love to you. But a few I would keep by me. I'd steal them, and we'd climb to the attic to smoke cigarettes. It would be dry and dusty there. Sometimes I'd look out the window and see you on the ground with your men; they'd be hanging on to your arms and your clothes, like lead sinkers. Then you would leave, one day, and for a message you'd send a tornado. It would come up suddenly, while everything was deathly still, and it would roll your chosen house until it splintered."

Annie took off her clothes and went to bed, with the shades up and the kitchen light on and the door half open. When Philip came in, he found she had kicked off all the covers in her sleep and was shivering so that her teeth chattered.

Chapter 4

APHELION

Then they caught a condor, but it turned out to be female and had to go back to the wild.

Philip and Joan were in what struck him as a peculiar period of abeyance—akin, he thought, to what young couples in the era of marriage-as-sacrament must have felt before the banns were posted. Between themselves, they had worked out the basic structure of practical arrangements, but they had not given each other license to act differently in the eyes of the community. Joan would keep the house for the summer and the rest of the year, while he first traveled slowly back East with Annie and then returned to live in Urban's house with the dog Rupert while Urban and Harriet were in Florida. Joan would take Emily for the summer, but couldn't promise past August, and Philip said he wanted her anyway. Beyond that fall, they did not lift the curtain, at least not with each other. Once, Joan began, "When we're divorced . . ." but it was about buying a new car, which had few ramifications.

Trapping the condor solidified their plans, or so it seemed; discovering its sex changed them.

"We've named her Teresa," Joan said to Philip over the phone.

"You're sure it's a girl?"

"Same blood test they used on Topa. It's proven infallible with Argentine condors." From Joan's voice he might have thought Argentine condors differed only slightly from Nazi pigs.

"So, you'll try again."

"I'm so tired of it." Joan's voice on the line, always fuzzy from the phone at the refuge, seemed to come from across an ocean. "I sat there looking into her cage, after I heard, and she looked back at me like a stupid old shrew. You know the kind— too beaten down to be clever or malicious, too lonely to be kind. Her wings were pulled up against her neck, the way they do, like hunching an old pair of shoulders, and her neck and head just looked sore, with all that red skin, like she'd been flayed. I despised her."

"All that because she was female? Not her fault."

"All that because I need a break from it. I'm getting superstitious—I think I'm jinxing the project."

"Nonsense. They need you."

"They can spare me for a while. There's a fellow visiting here— I think I told you about him once—who's got a grant to study seagoing murres. They'll be leaving from Point Reyes after the breeding season next month. He can take on one more. And Phil, I have to get away."

That night they hashed it out, all the professional pros and cons for Joan, just as they had always done for each other. The expedition would last two months; while the Condor Recovery Team would hurt for her absence, they had two summer interns and three months left on the grant after September. "I have to pursue something besides lost causes," Joan said over her hot brandy, sitting across the table from him as she always did.

"Sure you do," Philip agreed, the double meaning hitting him a second later.

"I can take Emily still. I *think*. They've got no objection to her, that is, but if she's unhappy, I don't want to chain her to me."

"So play it by ear. You know I'll take her if you want. I'll come back to Newhall."

"I know you're happy to have her. Just think, that was what I wanted, once. Anyway"—Joan smiled wisely—"she likes you more than me."

"Not so."

"Oh, yes. She told me. You watch her cheerlead, and you promised to take her fishing."

"I'll make good on that promise."

"Do you remember, Phil—" Joan was cupping the brandy glass with her hands, staring into it as into a crystal ball. "Year before last, when you were baby-sitting Emily after playschool?"

"Go on."

"You left at some point. Didi came home from school and found her lying by the swing set screaming. She'd done it trying to jump off the swing like the big kids she'd seen, and she hit the metal post and sprained her knee. Bruised her head pretty badly too. We never knew where you were. You looked pretty white, though, when you got to the emergency ward, and I remember how your hands trembled, touching her knee."

Philip shook his head at the memory. "I was terrified. Anything could've happened."

"Where did you go that day, Philip?" Joan looked up from the glass, as if she'd found the question inside it. A scarf held back her hair, gypsy-style. "You never told us."

"I don't remember."

"Were you with a woman?"

"I honestly don't know. I recall before I left telling Emily to stay in her room, not even to go downstairs, that I'd be back soon. Obviously I was gone a lot longer than I'd thought to be. But where, or why . . . it's a blank, Joan."

The question hung in the air between them. Upstairs, Emily lay asleep; Didi was out somewhere, out later and later each night. "Anyway, it was irresponsible, isn't that the point?" Philip said. "You know now I haven't been faithful. What's it matter if that time it was a woman or an argument with Jack?"

"If it was an argument with Jack," Joan answered evenly, "you'd remember not to have one again while your child was unattended at home."

"I told you I've forgotten the reason I was gone. But it hasn't happened again. Remember, I raised her as my child, Joan. I was very careful—about a lot of things."

"Oh, you're right, you're right, you're right." Joan rose to pour the brandy down the sink. Her back to him, she said, "I know you're good with her. I guess I just wanted to squeeze a confession out of you. I haven't let myself be jealous, you see. So I play the protective mother. Jealousy is so humiliating."

"No, it's not." He rose and went to touch her arm, but she shrugged him off, her soft shoulder twitching instinctively away from his hand. He left the kitchen and climbed the stairs quietly to peek into Emily's room. She lay on her stomach, her mouth flattened against the pillow, a beanbag frog crushed under the weight of her arm. The cat she was allergic to was curled at the end of the bed; he lifted it gently and shooed it from the room, then laid the blanket over her and tucked it in loosely up to her waist. She stirred in her sleep and mumbled.

"I'll never do it again, babe," he whispered to her, and bending down, pressed his lips to her warm temple, where the blond hair lay like down and he could feel the vein pulsing with her heartbeat. He switched on the nightlight and left the room, propping the door ajar so that from the hallway, at least, he could hear the slightest sound.

◇   ◇   ◇   ◇   ◇   ◇   ◇   ◇   ◇

During their last weeks at Newhall Philip came by often, and always when he was there he spent the night in Annie's narrow bed. Though she had finished his robe, even the quilting on the collar and cuffs, it continued to hang in the studio, waiting for the right time. She had meant it as a farewell gift, a final gesture. Now was the wrong moment. So Philip still dressed in his street clothes when he got up in the morning to go home and shave.

The novelty had not even begun to wear off, but Annie wanted it to: she wanted them to fit easily together in the bed, like shoes packed and repacked in the same box. She was eager to replace one daily routine with another, not to remain in this middle state, where everything hinged on emotion.

Yet the nights he slept at home, she stretched out with pleasure to reclaim the bed. Sometimes she rubbed herself, not to reach orgasm but only to check that she was still there and had not been wholly replaced by the new version of Annie who was about to carry on her life. She lay still, on her back, one hand between her legs and the other behind her head, and looked out the window at the oak tree whose name she had only learned this year. She was in many ways ignorant, this Annie that Annie remembered. She pretended more than she knew, a useful trick in the theater. Not so useful elsewhere: her thesis had been no more than a spewing out of ideas on creativity that had lacked the natural cohesion of creation itself. Philip hadn't said so, but she read it over and knew. The old Annie had plunged into the subject without mapping out her territory, and the new Annie, about to be Philip's Annie out in the world, mourned her clumsy instinct-following sister. The sudden change had left her no time to complete a cycle, to create this world for herself.

But now, in the gap between exams and commencement, Philip could come by, since everyone knew, and everyone asked where were they going in the summer and what did her parents think. Their numbers were few, the ones who talked; just enough to make Annie feel herself on a dissecting table. Jack, she knew, reported that everyone was acting a little sorry for Joan, but since she wasn't fighting, they had decided it was for the best. It had always been a loveless marriage, he said—Philip had been unhappy for years and stayed only for the girls. Urban Whittaker no doubt put in that they had been a fun couple once, and always good companions for each other, but he had to recognize it had become a rut. While Keith's boys, at a final campus blast, would agree that it was totally fantastic but fraught with bad karma, and they had all seen right through Annie from the start.

Annie avoided them all, even the unsuspecting ones like Dave Prince, who was heading back to Detroit and wanted to know would she be there any time that summer. She denied the possibility, loudly, in case anyone within earshot thought they knew her plans. She hoped they—whoever they were—didn't actually see her lover mounting her steps late in the afternoon. It embarrassed her to receive him openly; she thought how others could picture them making love, and she no longer wanted even to meet Philip for coffee or walk with him over the campus.

"It's so obvious we're meeting to have sex," she complained.

"You act like you've been accused of fornication."

"Worse, my love. Adultery."

"For me, not for you."

"I know the people around here. They undress us in their minds and watch us screw."

"Do you do that to couples you know?"

"No, but their relationship hasn't been a secret. They haven't been found out."

"Neither have we. We came out."

He told her she imagined things. But what had been passionately unavoidable to Annie now seemed lewdly chosen, and her room not an intimate hideaway but cramped quarters for a bed.

For two days after drinking the gin, Annie could keep nothing down. Her stomach bucked against her as if it would heave her back from the steps she was taking. She would have liked to be alone, to tame it, to will it quiet again. But Philip spent both nights with her, nights which yielded little sleep. He made no comment when she spoke about Mona; Didi, in recounting his own secret to him, hadn't told him everything. His attentions were cheerfully given, with an insouciance that Annie found out of character.

"I just hope your sense of breeding doesn't object to my coming by four times today," he said.

"No. you're here to nurse me, not to jump in the sack. But let's leave as soon as I'm better, okay? I'll return to normal away from here."

"As soon as you're ready. Joan leaves for Point Reyes tomorrow, and I think Didi's eager to have the place to herself."

"Joan's taking Emily?"

"For now."

Annie searched his face. "Will it be hard, saying goodbye to them?"

"It'll be hard. Joan said a funny thing to me yesterday." He shook his head in nostalgia. "She reminded me we'd spent our first date watching birds. Both of us with our binoculars, peering through them as if we were blind without them, tapping each other's shoulder but not turning our eyes away from this visual prey of ours. She pointed out she was still doing that. As if I'd frozen her in time."

"You were twenty-five when you married her."

"And I'd slept with exactly two other women."

"Why? Did you marry her, I mean."

"Oh, the usual reasons. I wanted a family. I loved Joan. I still do." He lifted Annie's chin with his finger. "But we said goodbye a long time ago, really. And this remains an experiment."

"Sure, but it's still a big change in your lives."

Annie still felt herself the outsider when it came to Joan. Everything she said sounded trite and ignorant—she wouldn't know "the usual reasons," for instance. If only she could confront Joan herself, she might know what to fear and what to hope for; she might learn why Philip had chosen her, Annie. But Joan was leaving, taking a part of Philip with her which she would always keep. Little Emily would never bring the shards of the past to Annie, and Didi . . . Didi had erected a wall of silence, behind which she was sorting out her own means and ends.

"Not that it's my business," Annie went on, unable to let it go, "but are you so sure of Joan? Sure she's taking this as easily as it seems, without even flinching? She's so *reasonable*, I wonder if there isn't something going on inside, that even you wouldn't notice."

"Goddamn it, Annie! There are always things missing!" She had touched a nerve. Good. He rose from the edge of the bed and took some steps around the room, one hand on the back of his neck, the other gesturing as if the walls were an audience. "But finally—well, finally, you've got to act. I see no other way, do you? Look." He sat down again and took her hand. "Details about Joan and me don't have anything to do with you. But I am forty-six years old, and I haven't done anything completely as I wanted for twenty years. That's almost as long as you've been alive. Even with women, even you, there's been this restraint, this distance. It comes from worrying about how much I know, what I'm sure of. You wonder if I see deeply into Joan. Do you see deeply into me? You can't! Because I've scuttled it so thoroughly away, even I can hardly find it anymore."

"I feel it. In bed."

He smiled, then concentrated on her hand. "Yes, you do. But that's just sex, just a channel. It doesn't last after."

"No, you're right. It doesn't."

Philip's actions, like his thoughts, had always taken clear paths. Embryonic emotion was not something he acted on, or even nurtured. Now he was saying that the waters which bred his impulses were muddied, that he himself hid from her in the mud; but she would not believe him. He was only changing, and he needed her help. Of course. And he was taking the first step already, doing what he wanted, by going away with her, Annie. They would throw their lots together, like ordinary people. They would live in the everyday, asking everyday questions: Who would make the bed? What would they eat? What could they talk about? Was Emily coming to live with them? Did they have the same friends?

How trivial it is, Annie thought. Convalescing, getting ready
to leave Newhall, she looked for her specialness and found it
nowhere, and the ordinary things that filled her mind alarmed
her.

It was difficult for Annie to believe that Las Vegas had not been
through a war. Only on the manmade ruins of some holocaust
could people have built such flamboyant edifices; only in the
wake of destruction could abundance and chaos twist steel into
such bizarre and overgrown frames. The desert in its virginity
would never have tolerated such a weight of neon and metal,
paint and cement. It would have swept the imposter city off its
face.

And yet that was just what it had not done. Instead, the desert
had opened, making a kind of hole in its center that fit the city.
The city was not built on sand; it was built on nothing, while the
desert surrounded it and held it fast. The people walked alone or
in pairs on the streets which were built on nothing; the casinos
floated on a void and were supported only by the pressure of the
other massive buildings and of the encircling dunes. The feeling
one got of walking on a tightrope was hatched of the same
source. The sidewalk was not solid but only suspended from
invisible poles at either end of the strip, like a rope bridge. Philip
trod it with ease, but it gave Annie vertigo, which increased at
night when the sky was black but the lights washed out any stars.

But except for the imbalance it caused, she liked the headiness
of gambling and the funny, tawdry glitter. She liked, too, to slip
out of the room early in the morning, while Philip still slept, and
walk along the gray canal with the willows hanging motionless
over its side. The canal by day gave the city a new face, made it
simple and watery and connected to things.

The motel they had found in Las Vegas charged a weekly rate,
and the maid came in only every other day, which suited Annie.
It was on a back street, near the canal, and when they at last

returned for the night, the neon didn't penetrate the shades. The starched white curtains and still-life prints made an authentic effort at domesticity, and there was a small kitchen attached, which they used for breakfast.

When she got back from walking, Annie made breakfast and served it on a tray—a cold roll and coffee for herself, poached eggs for him. She loved to sit cross-legged on the bed as the late-morning sun came insistently through the curtains and to litter the sheets with crumbs and spilled coffee. They filled the time with superficial questions—How did you sleep? What did you dream about? Where should we go today? Then Annie cleaned up and they went back to bed. It seemed they would always want each other—even immense satisfaction lasted only until their bodies cooled, then desire returned. "You never tire," Annie said.

"Oh, yes, I do. Give me a few months of this." He pulled her hips toward his mouth.

They spent the day in the town or driving over the desert, and ate other meals in restaurants. Again she wondered: if later he would expect her to cook, to clean as Joan had—to be a mother to Emily if Emily came to live with them. But the questions seemed irrelevant in Las Vegas and soon passed, and she knew herself to be special again.

It had been Philip's idea to come here. "Las Vegas is a good place to decide things," he had said. "Life is very basic there, and very detached. Nothing afflicts the heart. It can go the way it chooses." And so as soon as Annie could leave Newhall, they had driven east across the desert. She had written her parents telling them not to bother about graduation, it meant so little these days, and she had met a nice young man with whom she'd be traveling. She had asked if she and the young man could spend some time at the family cottage in Wisconsin. Mrs. Redfield had replied that they would like to meet the person first, and that she would be there in July if Annie and her beau wanted to drive up.

"I've got to tell them," Annie had said, back in Newhall.

"No, you don't. We'll tell them when we see them. What's the matter, don't you think they'll like me as a 'beau'?"

"My mother's closer to your age than I am."

"Has she got a nice figure?" It wasn't funny, and Annie didn't laugh. "Well, let's not go, then."

"We can see." And so they had suspended everything, to decide once they were together in Vegas.

And in her walks by the canal Annie did feel a decision coming on, presaged by that vague sadness that foretells change. She did not know what the decision was, nor whose. Alone in the morning, a mingling of anxiety and anticipation propelled her until she was walking rapidly along the banks. Philip was not the teacher now. She could not come to him young and foolish and frightened and have her ghosts laid to rest. In bed he was tender, but what comfort he gave was hard, matter-of-fact. She had wanted it that way; she had let him think her old and crafty. Now she was losing that control that had buoyed her up and made decisions almost by itself.

She had had it all planned, she reminded herself. This life together, this miraculous daily intimacy—this was to have remained a dream.

Returning to the room mature and courageous, smart and cheerful, Annie made love with a ferocity that Philip remarked was extraordinary for a woman in the morning. Did he like it that way? Oh, yes, he did. He loved it. Her.

◇   ◇   ◇   ◇   ◇   ◇   ◇   ◇   ◇

The women in Las Vegas were either too old or too young. The old women sat next to miniature slot machines and stared out of grimy coffee-shop windows, while the young ones walked by, clinging to their escorts' arms because the stilletto heels they walked on wouldn't support them. The youngest filed in and out of the little white chapels in Glitter Gulch wearing their sheer white dresses or their tight blue jeans and halter tops, their bare skin goose-bumped in the chill desert night air. Sometimes they scurried to the altar in smocks, with an arm holding back their bellies; then they emerged, blushing, into the eternal daylight of the street. Their men were long-necked, drawling suckers with shiny black shoes, or else (but this was in the casinos) they wore toupees and drank scotch and kept one hand on their child-woman of the night. These older men bothered Annie. When they jerked their pelvises on the dance floor, it was as though they were pounding away at a soft, heavy woman who had pressed them to the wall so they had to thrust their way out. Or as though they were riding a man, or a dog, or the dead. When one of them would mount the hotel stairs still holding his girl as a mutt would its bone, Annie wanted to run and stop them, to push him back down the steps and rescue the smeary, drunken bride.

Everyone drank, all the time. Whiskey, gin, vodka, tequila: martinis, highballs, Manhattans, fizzes, margaritas. But while there were drunks on the street, in the casinos the liquor seemed to have lost its potency. Annie was astonished at how much she was drinking and how much she could hold. Liquor took the place of food, and still the sensation of floating over the sidewalks served more than drink to warp one's perception of the world. Alcohol only dulled smells and sounds, so that the press of people and the din didn't send anyone home.

Philip gambled, and won. After almost a week in Vegas he had won twelve hundred dollars playing blackjack. Annie gambled a little, won, then lost. She quit the roulette table and wandered around the hall, recording faces and conversations. Because someone inevitably hustled her, she stayed within sight of Philip. Once, sitting alone on one of the rococo couches which faced the wall of mirrors in the long hall, she was offered two hundred bucks for a trick. "It'd just take a minute," the man whined, twitching but hardly moving his lips. He was no more than thirty, but gaunt and sickly. Later, Annie would tell Philip he was the ugliest man she'd ever seen.

"Please go away," she said. He had started to sit down. "No, please don't sit there."

"Why not?"

"Because if you sit there I'll have to get up and move, and I sat down because I'm tired of being on my feet. No, please don't do that." He had taken a seat at the far end of the couch and was inching his way coyly toward her.

"I just won it all, and my pants is poppin." Before he could get within grabbing distance, she rose wearily and shouldered her bag. She considered hitting him with it, but he looked as if a blow would kill him.

I am Philip's girl, she would try to say with her hard eyes as she crossed the casino floor. And sometimes it worked, and they watched her make her way past the bar to her own graying man, whose hand traveled up her thigh, then released her.

◇   ◇   ◇   ◇   ◇   ◇   ◇   ◇   ◇

Urban Whittaker's father had left him a small cabin on a lake not far from Boulder Springs, Colorado, and Urban told Philip they could use the place as their next stop-off, if they wanted. "I'm not planning to be there before August," Urban said when he arrived in Las Vegas with Harriet for the weekend, "at the earliest. It's just a shack anyway, out in the woods. No phone, no heat except the fireplace. Just got electricity in last year. There's a tub bath, but no shower. Not really my style at all—I've been thinking of selling it for a place at Newport Beach."

Philip was glad to see Urban. They descended to a bar at noon, leaving the women above ground. "So Jack hasn't changed his mind," said Philip.

"Not a single notch. Why should he? I read his manuscript. It drips with porn, but it should make a bundle. And Ruth's moved out of Edgar's and in with Jack. They've got the advance—sonofabitch showed me the check. The lucky couple." He pulled on his cigar. When Jack had announced, at the poker game, that he had sold an erotic novel and didn't plan to teach philosophy again ever, they had both taken the news with a rock-sized grain of salt. "But that's what he's been up to, the past two years," said

Urban. "No wonder he's dysfunctional in the classroom—he's restricting his performance to the sack."

"Who's in this book?"

"Himself and Ruth, mainly. Edgar gets in there with his Hindu rituals of nonejaculation, which should give the book a great sales slant with the cults. It's a *tour de force* of steamy sex, I've got to hand it to the guy. He deserves the money. So what if he can't lecture anymore."

"But he can," said Philip, recalling Jack's class.

"I should tell you, by the way. There's a student in this book. A coed from Michigan. Fresh as new hay when she arrives on the scene, but she gets mown down pretty quick."

"By Jack."

"By our virile narrator himself."

"It's his fantasy, Urban. Everyone's known that."

"Just thought I should forewarn you. Wouldn't want you to see it in print without knowing."

They sat and smoked for several minutes, saying nothing. The bar was for daytime drinkers, regulars who didn't want slot machines or juke boxes or electronic games with their highballs. Sawdust covered the floor, reminding Philip of the Cattleman, which made him think of Didi, alone back at Newhall.

As they ordered a second round, Urban said, "I've been at this too much, Phil."

"What, the bottle?"

He nodded and shrugged. "It's having to face Harriet. I sent that girl home. Literally. She wanted to stay in Newhall and work at the drugstore and screw me. Now it's just waiting for the cycle to come round again."

"Why don't you end it, if it's that bad?"

"You are preaching a new gospel." Urban stubbed out his cigar. "But you know how it's been. You have to keep going back. Go back again and again and keep trying. Like Sisyphus and the rock." He chuckled, a guttural sound from his throat. "Who knows? Maybe you'll convert me. Or I you."

Philip said nothing.

"Think about it. Maybe it was just Jack's fantasy," Urban went on, leaning across the table. "But there's another Jack out there, pal. He'll claim her. And Joan's a lovely woman. You need this affair, sure. But you don't want to lose Joan."

"I have. Already. Lost. Her." Philip left space between each word to make sure Urban had heard him rightly. He had no wish to preach.

"Well, then, I'm sorry. And like I said, the cabin's yours for the asking," said Urban, finishing his drink.

"Good enough. But let me return a piece of the favor. You found a place to stay yet?"

"Hell, no. Our stuff's in the car."

"Take our room for a couple of nights. We've paid up for two weeks, but Annie's been wanting to see the Grand Canyon. I could drive her down this afternoon."

Lost her. For the first time, leaving Urban below in the bar while he escaped to find Annie, Philip felt the blow of the loss and, as he hit the wide, bleached street, the blank tablet of the future. Distinction and fame he had tucked casually into his back pocket; genius, he knew, lay out of his grasp. But he had had Joan. All of her. She didn't give herself away in parts, and she didn't take herself back that way, either.

"For never can Happiness and the longing for what is not exist together. For Happiness must have all its will." That was Epictetus, the old goat, whispering to him over the blare of the car horns, the tinny shouts of barkers, that he had known it all along.

It was easy to straighten up the room, pass the keys to Urban and Harriet, and drive down the heat-slicked highway to the Grand Canyon. The desert, so close, proved a welcome relief from the surreal city. Most of the flowers had faded, but the stark hills rose steadily up from the plain, and mirages gleamed silver in the sun. The air was dry and clean. They reached the canyon by three o'clock, with six hours left before dark, and Annie wanted to hike down the trail.

"We haven't got the right shoes," Philip said.

"Just a little ways. Come on."

"You'll see a lot more from the top, believe me. There are woods to obscure the view going down, with bugs in them."

They took a shuttle bus around the rim, stopping every five minutes at a viewpoint. Standing apart from the crowd, Philip pointed out the geologic peculiarities of the rock strata. "See over there, where the lower layers slant upward while the top layer is level? That's the Algonkian Wedge—the Precambrian part is tilted and beveled, but the Cambrian came much later and was formed at a normal horizontal."

"You never stop being a teacher, do you?" she teased.

"Do you mind?"

"No—though I'm not a very good student. I can confess, now that I'm through with it. I like to hear you tell things, but I don't remember them."

"Good, so long as I don't become a bore."

They stayed the night at one of the cabins attached to the lodge that hugged the rim. The dinner the lodge served was bland and hearty, unlike anything they'd had in Vegas, and afterward Philip, who had gambled into the early hours for six nights running, went back to the cabin to read while Annie took a walk.

She always asked him to come with her on walks, and he usually turned her down. When he did come along, he would begin to breathe hard after about twenty minutes and suggest they turn back. He seemed middle-aged then, and his age a weakness he indulged. Still she asked, as if not to ask were to forfeit him the option of being young. But it was better when he refused.

A country band was playing bluegrass in the courtyard, and the day's hikers were expending their last energies, stomping their feet and dancing. Annie looked on, wishing she could join. Her muscles were cramped from the car and bus. She had hardly walked a mile that day. But when two hikers in jeans started toward her, she slipped out of the circle into the night. How explain to them that she was "with" someone? That it was not someone of their sort, in a lumberjack shirt and boots, but a kind man who asked for your last name? At Newhall Philip's age had been invisible. He had mixed with students, he had danced at parties, he had smoked pot, he had shown up at rallies to protest Vietnam. But there had been a code by which Annie's friends had lived, and he didn't follow that code. These people lived by that code too, and here outside academic walls he couldn't fit in with them.

And then as she walked away from the light, Annie felt the same nausea that alcohol had brought on, the day of Mona's visit to the studio in Newhall. Who was she to call shots, and out of what fear? She let Mona love her, she tempted Philip to make sacrifices for her—and then she said no. No further. She felt the urge to scheme, to hang on to him without giving up her youth or letting him share it. It was she, more than his actual age, that could deny youth to him if she wanted to—if she wanted to treat her love for him like a sickness, a vice she could allow in part so long as it didn't contaminate her whole self.

"But why?" Looking over the rim out of sight of the lodge, she spoke aloud to the canyon, and it swallowed up the sound. "Why not grow?"

That was the point, wasn't it? To nurture the love until the rest no longer mattered? But then, echoed another voice, if it dies. On the wide path at the edge of the crevice Annie stood and rained her fists upon her face. Because she didn't know what was alive or dead, or what she wanted to kill, or why, or if she could breathe into things any life which was not false.

Checking tears, she turned back. By the time she reached the room the thing which had seized her had passed. Vapors, she said to herself. She smiled at Philip, asleep in his chair, and when she knelt down and woke him, he reached for her breast. They looked happily and wisely on each other, as do people in whose closeness there are no more secrets.

When they got back to Las Vegas Philip called Didi. "How does she sound?" Annie asked when he had hung up.

"Good. Says she's spending time with Ruth and Jack. Wants to know how we're getting along. I imagine she wishes the honeymoon were over."

"She despises me, doesn't she?"

"She'll come around."

Next he called Joan to check on Emily. She was fine, Joan reported—loving the seashore, there was a play group every day, Philip shouldn't have to worry about her the rest of the summer. "Are you sure?" Philip kept saying. "We could work it out, if you're not sure." Then she put Emily on, and he told her he'd see her before she knew it and to have lots of fun.

"They're going to take the kids out on the beach the night the murres head out to sea," he told Annie. "Should happen sometime next week, at the full moon. It's an incredible sight. A whole cliff face covered with month-old chicks and their fathers. The mothers will be out foraging when they do it—just launch off the cliff into the water, hundreds of them, never to return until they nest again. They scream to each other as they go off, babies calling to fathers, fathers to babies. Gulls gather to pick off the laggards. A real crowd scene. Later on, the mothers come back, fish in their beaks, all perplexed. I'd give anything to see Emily's face when those chicks jump." Smiling, he rubbed Annie's knee, then went to mix a drink in the kitchen. Annie followed him.

"You know," she said, "when you go back, it'll be to them."

"Who, the murres?"

"No. Didi and Emily. You're addicted to your daughters, Philip."

"Who says I'm going back?"

"Okay, *if.*"

"When a man wants more, he has to take less somewhere."

"I'm not more anymore. I'm just different."

"I don't understand. You don't seem pleased."

"I'm sorry, Philip, it's just . . . I'm reading into the bird story, that's all. I didn't mean anything." She leaned against the counter; touched his sleeve. "Let's get out of here, okay? Even if it is a good place to make decisions, the decisions can still be wrong."

"Urban's invited us to his place in Colorado."

She shook her head no.

"Well, where do you want to go?"

The first thing that came to mind was "back to Newhall," to her studio and her sketches and the fabrics she could run through her hands, but that time was past. Next she thought, "to New York," but it was too soon to say it—September was a lifetime away. They hadn't really talked; they had decided nothing. And there was nothing for Philip in New York. And nothing for her in Newhall.

"What do *you* want to do?" she repeated back to him.

◊   ◊   ◊   ◊   ◊   ◊   ◊   ◊   ◊

The robe for Philip was in a flat rectangular box, which Annie could just fit in the bottom of her suitcase. Packing clothes around it, she thought maybe she would wait until he noticed the box. Let him discover the gift. But he was not apt to pay attention to what went into her luggage, or to say anything if he did. He was not going to find the robe; he was not going to step in and take it from her. Yet something had gone into the making of the gift that she couldn't step forward to give to him. There existed something she was afraid to lose.

They were packing to head northeast. "We'll hit the road and see how it feels," Philip had said, waking early that morning, and Annie had mumbled, "Sure."

Urban gave them the keys to the cabin and a map, just in case. "Not really my style at all," he said again. "But you might come on the vicinity at nightfall and it'd be handy."

That evening they all met at a place that Annie guessed was more Urban's style, a dark grotto with a fountain, red vinyl booths, and candles in plastic molds shaped like bigger candles, with globs of preformed "wax" running down the sides. The menu had fancy sweet drinks and variations on steak and shellfish à la carte, all with gambling names like "Hold 'em Lobster." Philip and Urban discussed the honors convocation, the new dean, the faculty retreat, the tenure crackdown. Jack's book was good for a number of laughs. Harriet asked Annie how she liked Las Vegas, and wasn't it horrible how the men stared at you? Annie agreed, though she didn't notice any staring at Harriet. Harriet was wearing a silk pantsuit, violet, with huge printed flowers billowing over her breasts. Annie had on a long, slim sheath that highlighted her tanned neck and arms. The Latin waiter winked at her as he deposited curls of butter on their plates. No doubt he thought she was someone's niece, or a gold digger after Philip. How lovely to play the part.

But she wished they would order and get the evening over with. The sight of Philip with these two irritated her. How had he put up with them all these years? They were good-hearted but tedious, and at dinner Philip became equally dull, cracking the same jokes and making the same worn remarks about Vegas.

After dinner they went next door to a casino and bar with dancing. Harriet was already drunk, and Annie wanted to catch up with her. They sat at the bar with gin and tonics and watched the men melt into the crowd.

"He's lost weight, you know," Harriet was saying.

Annie swung her stool back to the bar. "Who, Urban?"

"Can't you tell?"

"Well, he does look more trim. Yes! I hadn't noticed."

"You know why? Because I told him he was better in bed when he wasn't a tub-tub, that's why. Appealed to the vanity of his cock. Not that I give a damn, now."

They got another round. "I want to dance," said Annie.

"Not with me, thank you."

"No, with Philip." It sounded like "fill-up."

"You're nuts about him, huh?"

Annie blushed, and Harriet leaned closer. "I don't blame you," she said. "You've made a new man out of him, too. Much better than that priggy little Joan. Urban and I had been hoping someone like you'd come along."

"I want to dance," Annie repeated. Sliding off her stool, she leaned against the bar for support, then shaded her eyes against the overhead lights to search for Philip. "See you," she said, and wove her way through the gamblers.

It was better away from Harriet. Feeling loose and giddy, she wandered past the tables, thinking Philip's name hard so she would find him faster. A lean, greasy man pinched her breast at the side, under the halter top, and she slapped him, clumsily. "Up yours, sister," he called after her.

She would kick them all off the tiny dance floor and step out, she decided. She would move. She would take hold of the smoky, rhythmic air and work off this torpor.

She found Philip at the blackjack table. Urban was behind him, playing craps. She tapped Philip on the shoulder, and when he looked up she grinned.

"Hi!" he said. "Want to play?"

"No. I wanna dance."

"Wait, I have to finish this game."

She sat down next to him and rested her cheek in her palm. The cheek felt hot. "I hate Harriet," she said.

"I know. She's tactless."

"It's not that. I just don't like her. I like Urban all right. He's always been decent to us."

"Urban and I have been talking. I'll tell you about it later."

"Can we dance now?" she heard the sloshy whine in her own voice. He looked at her.

"I think we should get you home to bed."

"I'm fine. I just need to move."

"Come on, then, let's get some air." He took her arm and propelled her outside, whispering something to Urban as they passed. When they hit the fresh air Annie felt her stomach begin to rise.

"Philip—honey—I'm going to be sick."

"Right now?"

She nodded.

"There are some bushes here. Okay." He held her shoulders as she bent forward and retched forth her dinner and the booze. It didn't last long. Hot tears stung her eyes.

"I'm so embarrassed."

"Nonsense. Let's get you home now."

"Urban and Harriet—"

"I told Urban."

"My sweater."

"I'll get it." While he was gone Annie sat on the curb, her face in her hands. She had spoiled the evening. She had been childish again, insecure, stupid.

Philip, the knight in armor. He returned with a glass of water, which she drank obediently. The water seemed to scrape against her throat, but it relaxed the spasms in her stomach. "I'm sorry," she said as they drove back. "That's twice it's happened."

"Don't be ridiculous. Anyone can get sick."

"Any teenager."

Back at the motel, she washed her face and mouth and got into bed beside him. "Let's just pet each other," she said.

"I'd like that." As if reading her mind he added, "It was a nervous evening for me, too."

"Yeah?"

They lay side by side and stroked each other's bodies with light, knowing fingers. Annie smoothed Philip's forehead where the eyebrows made a knot, and he traced her small spine.

"We have to talk," she said.

"We will. Now's not a good time."

"No."

He turned over. She curved her belly around his back and held him close with her free arm, the fingers laced into his chest hair. She was tired but afraid to shut her eyes. She blinked them open until the force of sleep overcame the muscles, afraid that when they closed, some world, a world she did not yet know, would vanish.

When Annie woke next morning, the last morning in Las Vegas, Philip was gone. Caught between sleep and waking, she reached for him in the wide bed, and a few minutes later reached again. The mattress was no longer even warm. She opened her eyes onto the ceiling; very slowly she turned her head and looked around the room.

But some of his clothes were still scattered on the floor, and there was no note neatly folded on the dressing table. He had not left her.

The humming electric clock read 8:15. Annie had no idea what time they had gone to bed but guessed it had been early. Her throat felt dry, her face warm. She rose and got a drink of water, cold and alkaline from the tap.

Her suitcase lay on the rack, fully packed except for toilet articles and last night's dress. Carefully, she lifted out the folded clothes and laid them on the bed, until she had reached the flat white box at the bottom. She pulled the robe out and shook it; the velour snapped and then floated back to the floor. Spreading it on the bed, she shaped the cloth as it would be when worn, with the sash tied carelessly and one arm bent inward at the elbow. Between the embroidered lapels she could see the flawless back seam and the facing to which she'd stitched a label—*Hastings Ltd.*—in case Joan were to ask. She thought back to the long nights at the studio, when the whir of the sewing machine had been the only sound in the building. She used to lose track of the time; it had seemed impossible to think of anything but Philip as she worked, as if the robe had demanded that single-mindedness in its construction. Now, perfected, it lay as her complete offering to him, the giving-over of herself.

And yet of course to him it would be just a robe, a beautiful robe. Studying the finished product on the bed, she pictured Philip as he would rise up in it and walk the length of the worn rug. She tried to believe he would comprehend how she had made herself vulnerable to him, as if the robe could whisper her secret. But in the end the nagging fear remained that he would see a silly piece of cloth made fancy. She didn't have the trust to give it to him, and from that lack she saw that she would not give him, finally, herself. She would not go the distance.

Quickly she folded up the robe and tucked it back into the box, then repacked the suitcase. He must not see it. She brushed her hair and went back to bed. When the key turned in the lock and Philip entered quietly, she was still on her back under the covers.

"I'm awake," she said.

"I've been for a walk." He removed his shoes, came to the bed, pulled down the covers, and began stroking her.

"I thought you'd gone."

"Gone? You mean left you?"

"Yeah—just for a minute, I did."

"And how did that feel?"

"I don't know," she answered truthfully. "I just thought, 'He's gone,' and then I lay here. I realized you hadn't, right away. The feeling only lasted a second."

But there had been hope. Face it. And a kind of peace—a relief to give up the dream. To keep the firelight, evenings home, winters in the mountains, delicious and untasted. Untried, like the robe.

"Well, I'm not gone," he said, and he bagan to caress her, as he liked to do in the morning. "What a crazy idea."

"I don't know—it just occurred to me like that."

"In fact," Philip went on, sliding his hand between her bent legs, "I have another plan of departure. For both of us." She squirmed and lifted her arms; his hand traveled to the delicate skin under them and in the curve of her small, flattened breasts.

"I don't get it."

"I've been talking to Urban. He said something last night about not needing a leave in the fall after all. We met for coffee just now and talked it over. It seems he and Harriet are getting a divorce."

Annie moved her elbow, stopping his hand.

"Inspired by us, it also seems. They saw no hope, in the end, of saving things through some desperate second honeymoon in Florida—they'd only have been at each other's throats with no one else for distraction. I think it's smart. They were much better friends with one another before they married—they'll probably get along after they separate. Of course, there aren't any kids to complicate things."

"I thought you said Urban was the kind who always went back to his wife."

"That was the tune he played two days ago. I told you Las Vegas changes things. Quickly, sometimes."

Annie thought of Harriet appealing to the vanity of her husband's cock. "Not that I give a damn, now," she repeated to herself.

"Hm?"

"Just something Harriet said."

"Anyway. With Urban staying around, the department doesn't need me next year," Philip went on, "and you and I could obviously stand an absence from Newhall. I've got royalties from my last book coming in, and I could foot a trip to England"—he was watching her face— "or somewhere else. We could leave anytime, and come back when we were ready. A month, six months, a year."

"And when we came back?"

"We could see, but I've been doing some thinking." He was warming up to his plans; his eyes shone. "You could get your degree at UCLA. You're a woman, and you have excellent credentials—you'd have no problem getting in. There may be an opening in the department in a couple of years, if Keith isn't reappointed."

"Which you'd see to."

"Not at all. Since I don't like him personally, I'd probably bend backward out of guilt to help him. But he's not a good teacher. He's niggling, he plays favorites, and his mind's in a cloud. Your work's been exceptional, and you'd be welcomed—not just by me. By all of us."

Annie flipped onto her stomach and looked at him sideways. He had reached a pause, and she gave the silence a moment. They had to move slower.

"Philip," she said at last. "I've told you I'm not a scholar. I'm clever; I do a good snow job. But I don't really care about books and theories and research. I'm not even very interested in truth. I'm not. Do you remember what I was planning to do before Joan found out and we left Newhall?"

"Something with the theater?" He was ready to make it a joke.

"Costuming."

"Far below your capabilities."

"It's the only job I've been offered. And it's not just a job—some people would give their right arms to get into the American Academy. I'd just be doing seamstress work at first, sure, but it would mean being in New York and traveling and maybe designing later. I have a flair for it. It's kind of a—an opportunity." She was embarrassed by her own worldly, ambitious voice. It was to have been the perfect antidote to this affair, when it ended: hard work, late nights, young people, a small studio downtown, friends, entanglements. Callow and trivial, in Philip's eyes. "I was thrilled when I first heard."

"You've told them no?"

"I haven't told them anything. I've got till August."

"Well, so do it. I've got some time coming to me in the fall. I could relocate. To tell the truth—this isn't the time to get into this, but it's come up, so I'll mention it—I've gotten pretty damn sick of Newhall College anyway. I don't know if it's the size of the place, or the people in it, or the whole academic circus." He grinned. "Sometimes I don't know if I'm that much of a scholar myself."

"Yes, you are." It's written all over your face, she thought. Learning, truth-seeking, abstraction, knowledge.

"I thought this trip to England might help me decide that, as well."

Annie felt her mouth tighten, like an obstinate child's. No trip to England. No.

"There's another thing. I called Joan, up at Point Reyes."

"When, this morning?"

"From the coffee shop. I didn't want to wake you. We had a long talk. Better than any discussion we'd had, face to face, since this happened. She wants a divorce as soon as possible. I said fine. And she said she wanted custody of Emily. Which surprised me."

Emily. Annie had forgotten Emily. "You said yes?"

"After a while."

"Why did it surprise you?"

Philip didn't answer. He was staring at the wall, his hand motionless on Annie's hip. They remained that way for a long time, with no sound in the room but their breathing and the hum of the air conditioner. Annie shut her eyes, then opened them. Was he going to answer her? She waited for a sign. Every few seconds the air conditioner clicked, as if ticking off the electricity it used.

She didn't know the mystery behind Emily; she didn't want to know. She wanted to keep ignorant of all bargains struck between Philip and the wife he had never complained of. She knew that Emily weighed somewhere in the balance Joan and Philip had achieved, but all that could matter to Annie was that the balance would always hang before her, beautiful in its symmetry, the symbiosis of marriage still unshakable. She could only fight Joan with the weapons Philip gave her, and he didn't even acknowledge the battle.

But Philip said no more about Emily. He was thinking about Joan. He saw her, suddenly, in the dark motel room at Point Reyes, half dressed, her bra strap twisted and pins still in her hair. She would have been massaging her feet, a habit she had while on the phone, rubbing the high arch to relieve cramps. Over the line her voice had been calm, almost meditative. Emily's allergies were under control, she had said, and she had a friend in the play group teaching her double cartwheels. Joan herself was lonely but not homesick—he knew she meant not lonely for him—she only wished someone would get her out so she wouldn't huddle in her room in the evenings. She sounded tired.

A sharp regret had hit Phillip intermittently over the last weeks. He reproached himself, not for letting her go, but for marrying her in the first place. Asking her small body to bear his children, nurse them, expecting her to put up with him—it seemed too much, he'd had no right to demand it. He'd given nothing back, not even fidelity, which should have been easy. And now something more nagged at him. He couldn't connect the voice of Joan on the phone with the body of Joan. Talking to the voice had not been talking to her. Something was missing; she was gone, a ghost.

To Annie, Philip looked old, as he always did when he was thinking hard. Over the lines that cut into his face between nostril and jaw his cheeks hung heavy and slack. She reached out her hand to smooth his forehead, but her fingers brushed skin dry as paper and she turned away. "Are you sick of it?" she asked.

"Of what?"

"Never mind." She let the silence in again, then raised herself on her elbow. She stroked the sheet with her fingers, imagining his flesh. "Philip, I've decided something," she said. He looked at her without focusing his eyes. "I didn't realize I had until now, but I have."

He wasn't waiting for her to go on. He wasn't listening. She changed her mind—she had to see first, to test the old attraction. "Let's make love."

"Hm?"

"Make love to me."

He smiled as if she had made a small joke, and his hands began to move again. "You're funny. Such a sweet body." You always say that, she thought, and always with sadness.

He stood up and undressed with his back to her. Unbuckling his pants, he slipped them off and dropped them neatly over the back of a chair. Then he knelt between her legs and massaged her belly. "What did you decide?"

"Ask later."

"No, tell me now."

She tilted back her head to look at the ceiling. The plaster was flaking off. "I feel bad enough about the mess I've already made."

"Don't play the martyr. If you don't want to live with me, say so."

"But I do. I dream about it." The dreams were unclear, warm and hibernative, with the two of them inside a cocoon so dark she couldn't see his face. She could feel herself growing moist. "I was—strong," she said, "and I was sure of myself, when I thought I'd have to leave you behind. All this weakens me, now. I hadn't planned on it."

"I am asking you to change your plans." He tilted her pelvis and pushed back her thighs. "I changed mine." As he entered her, very slowly, she felt the blood start down from her lips. His mouth was on her nipple, wet and powerful. She was a bit of charmed wreckage, buoyed by the urgent wave.

You are old you are old the bottoms of your trousers rolled. The awkward way you dance. You tire after a walk. The visible ballast of your stomach.

A robe. To lift the robe from your naked shoulders. Under your arms, the soft skin like a baby's smells of soured cream and salt. Between your legs, stepping out of the robe as out of a sea, the same scent.

Philip stopped moving. She felt him inside her like a voice calling, and she wanted him desperately, wanted nothing else. "There's no reason," he said.

"Don't talk." Gripping him with her heels, she pulled his head down to her chest as if to still his words and so hear the voice she wanted.

But he jerked his head up and made her look at him. His face, twisted, pushed itself at her. His jaw hung open. Then he began to move again, fast and violent, the roughest he'd been. As Annie's head hung over the side of the bed, she cried out. Sweat covered them both. "Say yes," he whispered.

"I'm coming." She felt it rising in her then, lifting her off the bed and into him.

The beauty, here.

They finished. Annie felt the lid of her life shut quietly and neatly, like a cardboard box. Philip lay without speaking, his face pressed against the mattress, his body very warm, heavy and still.

◇   ◇   ◇   ◇   ◇   ◇   ◇   ◇   ◇

His head propped on both pillows, Philip was smoking the sixth in a succession of cigarettes. He let the ash burn to a long and dangerously drooping end, then dropped it somewhere near the ashtray. His mouth felt dry, as if he wanted a drink, but within the dryness lay the urge to speak—the air pushed against the roof of his mouth, curling his stymied tongue. He could not move to get a drink, nor could he open his mouth to make contact with the naked woman packing her clothes in front of him. He swallowed dryly, his saliva bitter with tobacco. He didn't know the language that would retrieve her, or else he had forgotten. Or else she had, and he couldn't make her remember, not even in bed. Something had struck them both dumb.

Annie bent to pick up articles and reached to check shelves with a suppleness he believed he could watch for hours. In the heat her slight, erect body had the bearing of a primitive, the nipples tilting upward, the belly barely rounded, sure and powerful. The nakedness itself had a fiendish quality, a design. Twice he opened his mouth to ask her to put something on, then remained stoically silent. They had said nothing for ten minutes. The packing was nearly done.

Annie wanted to be alone. She groped for a way to reverse her course, to stop these movements. A sudden chill in the heat, maybe, to slow her like syrup. She had hoped that nudity and silence would frustrate him so that he would go out for a while, but he stayed and followed her with his eyes while the rest of him lay still. Her hands as she tucked the last things into the suitcase touched the box with the robe. There it lay, like a genie in its bottle, ready to give her over completely, to drown out the reasonable, well-modulated voice directing her so sanely: "Pack. Leave. You are going to New York. You are not Philip's girl. You have outgrown this." The genie would pull her, in the old debate she had had while eating a doughnut in Santa Monica, back to the broad bed where nothing else mattered, back to Philip, who had changed his plans for her.

But he wouldn't have understood the sacrifice. There was no trough in his heart into which she could dump her soul. And what could she do for him, even in a gift? Leaving was the most generous act she knew—so she told the genie.

The voices of her thoughts confused her in the silent room, and again she wished he would go out. They had already agreed on the details. Philip had roused himself after what seemed like an eternity of lying dead-still in the morning heat while she, her eyes fixed on her lover, had slowly, deliberately denied the rich satisfaction that always welled up afterward. She could feel it rolling out, in slow waves from the core of her body, ready to rush to her eyes and fingertips. Stopping it up gave her a headache. Then she closed her eyes and sensed the decay nascent in him. His muscles, in the strong upper arms she had loved to stroke, had ripened and annealed; next, they would calcify into the knots of old men. She had laid a hand on her own smooth thigh, moist with sweat.

He lay so still, so long—at one point when she looked at him, heavy and white, she thought he was dead. No, unconscious—a heart attack, men could get them young if they smoked and drank. Even at forty they were vulnerable; he was nearer fifty. Then he turned his eyes on her from where he lay, and she knew they judged her. "We could still go on to Urban's cabin," she offered, "for a week or so."

"I know, but let's not."

She tried to smile at the irony. *We don't have to continue this,* she remembered his saying, at the start, and her *Yes, but let's.* It had been easy to say, easy to make the right motions. Now it was hard just to speak, and each step she took around the room landed wrong. And yet neither of them had changed.

Philip would drive back to Newhall. Annie was flying on to Detroit and the summer house in Wisconsin, where she would stay as long as she could put up with her family. Then New York. "It seems so funny," she said suddenly, breaking the long silence, "that we can do exactly what we want. I keep expecting something to stop us."

"You're not used to being free. We could only stop each other."

And you won't stop me, she thought sadly. "Have you decided anything about Joan?"

"Not a thing. You know, it's sort of curious"—now that he could talk, he went on as if to himself, or as if talking about himself, a disembodied observer—"what a habit the home is. Deserted by you, I head back as if there were nowhere else to go, when in fact the whole world is open to me and my fat wallet, and would probably be a damn sight more healthful for both." At the word "deserted" Annie started to protest, but Philip's voice continued, smooth and disinterested. The veil she had seen him pull about himself before now hung opaque. "But home is always so easy. It's seductive. Why not? you say. It's not like where I live, or with whom, is the crux of the matter anyway. And then you find your mind going back to what you do alone. Your 'higher calling.'" He laughed dryly. "Even if you remember, which you don't, that you had pulled that calling down from its height and thrown it on the shit pile. Because it's comforting to have its support and the environment that bred it. Sort of like an invisible, faithful dog."

"You could try something new."

"I'm no good at anything else. And once I'm back, I'll start recognizing responsibilities again. Emily, for instance, and Didi, who'll tug on my exposed heartstrings. I may try to leave, but I'll probably settle in again." He stopped to light another cigarette. "Or I may get brazen and try to win you back."

"Oh, I don't think you'll do that," Annie answered hesitantly. She didn't know whether she hoped he would or hoped he wouldn't. She wanted something to win her, yes.

"Your flight doesn't leave for a couple of hours," he said, finally getting up from the bed. "I think I'll take a walk. Want to come?"

"No, I've got to shower. Thanks, though."

Philip stopped on the bridge over the canal where he knew Annie had been taking her morning walks, and examined his reflection in the water. The oily sheen of the surface made his face look less like a mirror image than like a poorly developed photograph. The flesh appeared slightly purple, gray in the shadows, and the water's current distorted his features until he appeared a scowling old man, with pouched cheeks and an undulating forehead. Could this be how he looked to Annie? The idea was absurd, yet he stared at the face in the water as if apprehending the mask he wore for her. He picked up a pebble and dropped it in, shattering the image. As it cleared he wondered what a new surface would show. The face he still owned in his vain imagination, maybe, bold and smooth and searching? The water calmed and the warped image reappeared. No, the rippled creases ran too deep, they couldn't be erased. Even the touch of wisdom had aged and was no longer surprising.

Maybe she was right, to see him thus. Not that he was what anyone called old; that would be indulgent. He was just old enough. It wasn't that he'd thought himself young, either. He hadn't paid any attention to aging or to age, his own or anyone else's. But the body paid heed. It became pale and spotted and wrinkled and weighty and dead. He'd given himself the fancy that he was essential to her, that he gave her, not life, but the only life that made her whole. That no one else, especially no younger man, could give.

I know that, she was saying to her fate. It was not just his fancy. She would go on, inexpressibly whole, and no one would recognize her. And she wanted this! He could have spat on his body for pushing her to such a fatal mistake. It was an excuse, this mask she mistook for him, for her to run—not from age but from life. How stupid! How stupid for them both!

A small fat man walked by, leaning on a cane, exhaling garlic as he passed. Philip continued quickly down the ramp of the bridge and found the first open bar. He ordered a martini and a sandwich, and the red heat receded from his thoughts. He tried to imagine some way in which she was doing the right thing, some future in which profound and subtle differences would inevitably have separated them. It didn't work: in his future they fell together by that accident of nature called *simpatico*.

Nothing to be done now. She was gone, returned to the flock of her peers like a sheep, its unique markings buried in its wool.

And he, too, would return, but missing something. He closed off his face, his new fragility, from the smiling waitress and the businessman beside him. When the waitress brought his change, he put a quarter in the booth's miniature slot machine, out of habit. It turned up a banana, a peach, and a small boy making a face at him. He went back to the motel.

The shades were up, and he could see Annie dressing through the drapes. She had put on straight-leg jeans, a thick leather belt, and a checked shirt which she left unbuttoned just enough to suggest the soft skin of her breasts. These were her traveling clothes, her "tough chick" clothes, she called them. For the first time the outfit did not strike Philip as misplaced. When she disappeared into the bathroom to fix her face and hair, he opened the door noiselessly and slipped into the room. He was ready to be clever and cutting, if it came to that; easily turned phrases hung between his teeth. But returned to her presence, his mind slowed and could not grasp. The skeptical carelessness with which he used to accompany his actions, like a secret reserve of his soul, had fallen away, leaving him awkward and sincere, and knowing only that something was wrong, false, which he was without power to unmask. She was requiring some emotional stratagem from him, and he was not used to being strategic in that way. For the first time he wished she were older and more used to linking actions with consequences.

Emerging from the bathroom, tightening her belt, she bumped right into him. "Oh," she said with the softness brought on by surprise. "You're back."

He took her in his arms and kissed her roughly. At first she forebore, as if she didn't want it but could hardly refuse the favor. He kept his lips there, and when she started to pull away, he held the back of her head with his hand. She would have to bite him to make him stop. Gradually her mouth gave way and opened, like a flower in the rain. He kissed her until she began to cry, then he let her go.

She had admitted the passion, nothing more. I am too simple a man, he thought. It was a fact others didn't accept from him, but it was true. A psychologist would soon have tired of him. His breaking heart, if that was what it was, wanted nothing more than the agent of its misery. No amount of mental sophistication provided another recourse. What understanding he had of her motives provided, like most understanding, neither acceptance nor action.

◊   ◊   ◊   ◊   ◊   ◊   ◊   ◊   ◊

"You don't think I can make it, do you?"

"Well, I've never known anyone who could. But we were just kids when we used to try."

"Tell you what—I'll make it over and back."

"Without coming up for air? Now that I don't believe."

"You forget I made the Michigan finals for long-distance."

"I remember that. But you were allowed to breathe between strokes."

"Okay—watch close, now!"

Dave Prince dived into the blue-gray water of the lake, sending up a spray that washed the dock and sprinkled Annie's back. She took off her sunglasses and wiped them with a towel. At first she could see Dave's body, skimming beneath the surface of the water, then as he got out to the float she could only detect the small stream of bubbles that reached the bobbing corks and arced back toward shore. Just as Dave became visible again, about two-thirds of the way back from the float, he let out a final burst of air and came up sputtering.

"Well, almost," Annie said. She was lying on her stomach against the warm, damp boards, her chin resting on the backs of her hands so she could watch.

"I ran into a mess of lake grass on the way out," he panted as he breast-stroked in. "Next time I'll be ready for that. I should be able to go all the way."

Annie pushed herself back onto her haunches and stretched, like a cat. "I'm going into the house," she said. "I feel like I'm getting burnt."

"The sun's not even out!"

"Yes, it is. The ultraviolet cuts through that haze, and that's what gets you. I can feel my back crisping, believe me."

Dave hoisted himself onto the dock. His olive skin had turned a moist, rich brown, without a trace of red. He had swimmer's muscles on his upper arms, but for the rest he was long and boy-skinny, and his cutoffs stuck to his thighs in wet folds. "You're just hot, that's all," he said. "What you need is a little cooling off."

"No, I don't want to go in the water, Dave. I just washed my hair, and this lake's so filthy, and—Dave!" He had grabbed Annie under the arms and was spinning her around. She had untied the backstrap of her bikini to lie in the sun, and now the bit of green cloth hung from her neck like a bib while her white breasts stood out against her red and freckled skin. "Dave! Stop it! I *really* don't want to go in! My suit—someone might be looking!"

"Who would look at us here?" he asked, laughing. His strong arms held her off the dock and began dipping her into the water. "Ready? One . . . two . . . three!" Tossing her out into the lake, he dived after her. When she came up, he kissed her before she could say anything.

"Not mad, are you?" he said. It was too deep to stand, and they were both treading water.

"No, I'll get you back, though." Annie managed, clumsily, to hook her strap in the water. "And I'm still going inside. I'll have to rinse out my hair."

His arms lifting against her thighs, Dave helped her onto the dock. "Are you staying out?" she asked.

"Yeah. I think I'll try for the float again, maybe clear out some of that muck growing out there."

"Okay."

Annie picked up her towel and sunglasses and headed back up the hill to the white frame cottage. The door to the screened porch which faced the lake yawned open; it had to be hooked shut to stay. The house had been built by Annie's grandfather on her mother's side, as a northern retreat for the family during the hot Mississippi summers. Made to accommodate a clan, it was mostly bedrooms—even the porch had cots—with a small den, a breezy, spacious living room, and a kitchen designed for snacks and chili-making on the gas range. Since its construction, the house had gradually been surrounded by similar retreats, but Mrs. Redfield's father had had the foresight to buy up six acres at a good price, including the small cove and dock, and the development on the other side of the pines was obscured from view.

The house was vacant, in the way only a house designed to hold summer-long crowds can be vacant—drafts seemed to wind through the bedrooms and down the long staircases, and the pine floors transmitted the sound of Annie's barefoot steps the length of the bottom story. She walked through the living room to the bar by the kitchen and got herself a lemon soda, then took off her suit in the downstairs bathroom and put on a terrycloth robe. Back on the porch, she sat cross-legged in the wicker rocking chair and watched Dave dive from the float.

Her mother had said nothing when she wanted to bring him up here. It had all been sudden and arbitrary, and Dave was too old an acquaintance for Mrs. Redfield to disapprove of him. Annie had flown home the last week of June and had learned the cottage would be free through the Fourth of July; two days later, she had invited Dave and was driving north with him along the west side of Lake Michigan. They had had sex, that first night, in an almost routine manner—as if they could skip the preliminaries by pretending they were already accustomed lovers. That hurdle past, they relaxed with each other. Dave was strong from sports, and surprisingly good as a lover. He knew tricks to set off Annie's orgasm; his technique was neat and foolproof, like flicking on a set of switches.

Annie liked Dave. He asked no questions and had accompanied her, it seemed, not without pleasure but mostly to oblige her. He would leave when she asked. He was capable of more than this pairing off, but he was lighthearted and did not push—he had had free time and was willing, that was all. Annie knew she would tire of him, but there was a wisdom in his simple acquiescence that she would miss. Would she shrug off the rest just as quickly? Could she not tolerate this easy acceptance?

Dave lay on his back on the float; she could see his body rise and fall with the even motion of small waves. He would swim back in when the sun fell below the tops of the pines, and they would drink beer or play backgammon. That night there was a new movie in the town; they might go, grab some hamburgers after, return home, have sex, and sleep. Next day they were planning to water-ski. Mrs. Redfield arrived on Sunday, and soon after that Dave would leave for Grosse Pointe. Annie's mother was bringing the twins, and while they played in the sand she would tell Annie how good-looking and bright Dave Prince was, and she would hint that it was all right with her if they had slept together, so long as they were discreet. Maybe, Annie thought, it will last a while. It could endure the summer, anyway.

She went back in to shower and change. As she undressed in the bathroom upstairs she caught sight of her body in the mirror. Except for the dryness of the burned skin and the white bikini patches, it looked the same as at summer's beginning. Her small breasts hung there, and the pelvic bone curved in the same way, as if it were indestructible. In another world, Philip Decker had charted this body and left his stamp on it. On the face, too, she thought, leaning closer to the glass. Like a picnic littered on the beach, the wine bottles and plates unchanged, her face accused her and challenged her to claim it as the same bit of debris she had left behind. She needed new features—nose, eyes, lips of her own. But these were her own.

She rinsed the slime out of her hair. No longer lethal with factory pollutants, the lake water remained oily and rank. Methodically she soaped her body, then remembered she had already bathed. Force of habit, she thought; no matter.

Dear Philip, she began in her head. *You would not believe the change in me. I wasn't quite ready before, but now I understand everything.* Scraps of stationery filled the wastebasket by her desk. Pieced together, they made a dozen similar beginnings.

Dear Philip, I have been a fool. . . .

Dear Philip, I have a new lover and he is a fool. . . .
Dear Philip, I was too young to know what I was doing. You never
realized how young I was. . . .
Dear Philip, I have aged years in the last weeks. . . .
Philip, I want you. Yours in fickleness, Annie.
Dear Philip, Are you back with Joan? . . .

Dear Philip, she began again in the shower, *Forgive me.* Then the
litany came into her head and she singsonged aloud: "But Thou,
O Lord, have mercy upon us, miserable offenders. Spare Thou
those who confess their faults. Restore Thou those who are
penitent."
Dear Philip, I am obsessed. I must have been crazy before. I've
always gone in the wrong direction. I think I was terrified by you. . . .
Annie stepped out of the shower and turned on the electric
wall heater. She stood before it and dried, then dressed in a loose
shirt and jeans. The light was already beginning to fail outside;
the haze had condensed into a cloud which blocked the sun. Soon
the air would chill and she would need a sweater.
Dear Philip, This is the hundredth time I have tried to write to you.
Why should I be afraid to say I love . . . ?
No good, she thought. He would hate a smarmy letter.
Dear Philip, There are six acres here, clean air, lots of birds—I don't
know their names. Good fishing, too. If you're fed up with me I could
introduce you to my mother. She doesn't approve of hard liquor in the
house, but there's a bar down the road. Nobody uses the study here—it's
got a huge oak desk and a manual typewriter, and you couldn't find a
quieter place to work. . . .
Annie heard the screen slam as Dave came in. He would forget
to latch it, and it would continue to bang in the wind. That
irritated her. I should be alone, she thought.
"Want a beer?" Dave called out.
"No thanks, I just had a soda."
"*Christ,* it gets cold when the sun goes down," Dave said as he
appeared at the top of the stairs. He disappeared into the bath-

room, came out with a beach towel, and popped open a Bud.
"Worse than California, I'd say."

"That's because it's damp. You feel it more."

"Look what I did to myself." Dave dried his back with the
towel, then turned around. A red scrape ran down the right side,
with drops of blood under the shoulder blade. "Some plant out
there doesn't like to be tampered with."

"Did you cut your hands, too?"

"No, it just laid this on me when I dived into a bed of it off the
float, to try and break the stuff up."

"Well, you should put something on it. Wait a second." Annie
rummaged in the medicine cabinet. "This should do it. 'Minor
cuts, scrapes, burns.' Stand here in the light." She rubbed the
white cream into the wound. "How does that feel?"

"Better. Takes out some of the sting."

Dave's back was long and thin, with snakes of muscle over his
shoulders and along his spine. Completely different from Philip's
back, it seemed still in a process of formation—more naked and
more ephemeral. *Dear Philip, You've probably figured it out already, but I just want to assure you that in leaving I deprived you of
nothing. . . .*

"Thanks," said Dave. He finished drying, stretching over his
tanned legs to get the feet.

Annie went back to the window. A few more clouds had appeared, and the western sky was charged with the intense blue
and white that preceded sunset.

"Wish I'd brought a robe or something," Dave was saying.
"It's only seven-thirty and that movie doesn't start till nine. I hate
wearing clothes when I don't have to."

"Don't wear anything, then."

"Too cold for that."

Annie had brought the robe, but it still lay in its flat box on the
shelf of her closet. She pictured it on Dave, the taupe enriching
his brown skin, his chest strong and hairless under the lapels. She
had already thought of giving it to him; it would be one way to

break the spell. But when in her mind she saw him belting the robe to his thin waist, when she thought of how he would sit and walk, the exchange became a violation.

Dear Philip, This is a gift I made for you at Newhall. It may sound silly, but I never had the guts to give it to you. Think of it as a part of me which I leave with you, since no one else will know that part. . . .

No. She wasn't giving it to Philip, either. It was too late.

"In early August, here," she heard herself saying, "you can see the northern lights."

"Will you still be here then?"

"I don't know."

Dave had come to stand beside her, in a flannel shirt and jeans. He smelled of the lake. She didn't want to look at him. When he touched her she felt barren, and as though she were filled with sawdust—not that his touch was dry or sterile, nor even that it affected her that way. It only made her aware of what was wrong, just as he might ignore the scrape on his back now, unless she touched it with her own warm hand. "When are you leaving?" she asked.

"In a few days, I imagine. Will you miss me?"

"Oh, I'll see you again."

"Do you want me to leave? You do, don't you?"

"No. Well, yes, in a way, I mean, it's been fun, but—"

"But you don't want me to take it seriously." He laughed. "I decided I'd start taking life seriously at age thirty-nine. Not before."

"No, it's not that either. I just want to be alone for a while. Don't you see?" She looked up at him, and saw her insistence going nowhere. "It's got nothing to do with you. I have to be alone. Can't you tell? I've got to be by myself."

"Okay, okay." The young man took her by the shoulders, his voice soothing as the breeze. "Take it easy. I'll let you alone."

◇   ◇   ◇   ◇   ◇   ◇   ◇   ◇   ◇

"The heat," Jack said. "It does something to your mind."

"Mind?" said Didi. "What mind?"

"That's exactly what I mean. You can't think when the temperature's over ninety. Even balmy weather distracts reasoning. Everyone knows the great thinkers came from northern climates—Hegel, Kierkegaard, Spinoza, Hume. Those guys had to pit themselves against the elements, so it was only natural that they should wrestle with internal challenge as well. Besides, they had more time indoors, and no TV. How many dedicated philosophers would leave this lovely picnic and hypnotic sunshine to go swelter over a lot of books? That's why they're doomed—your father might be famous, Didi-doll, but he'll never be great, not in this climate."

"It's perfect for writing dirty books, though, I hear."

"With the right inspiration, yeah. 'Course, it takes air conditioning to do the proper research." His eyes peeked over his sunglasses to twinkle at Didi.

"What do you say, Dad?" she asked. Philip looked up from the hamburgers he was tending.

"I say Jack's full of shit," he answered. "Was Plato inebriated by the Mediterranean Sea? Did Aristotle loll about on the sand? If anything, they had longer hours of light by which to work, and better health."

"They lived in a healthy society that didn't permit the decadence we indulge in."

"So move to Alaska."

"I should think you'd agree with me—I saw your rebuttal to Panacci in *Thought* this month. Survival of the fittest."

"That's not what you've got in mind. You people who advocate long wintry nights really have some notion of the ethereal soul, which can't exhibit itself when everything gets too warm and fleshy. Panacci's the one who'd agree with you. My point of view would hold that people in cold climates consume more alcohol, which kills brain cells."

"You seem to be killing off a few yourself."

"I've got too many. It's like bloodletting for me."

Philip opened another beer. The air was dry as an oven, and inwardly he agreed with Jack—thought in such climate hung limp as the leaves of a tender plant. He felt beaten down, stupid with the heat.

"We could try another float trip," said Didi.

"Just the three of us?" Philip asked.

"You could bring Emily."

"She's too young."

"You took me into the wild at that age. She'd love it."

"Forget it," Jack put in. "One dunking was enough." He was sitting next to Didi in a deck chair, shirtless and tan, the dark glasses concealing his eyes. For all his talk of heat, Philip noticed, he looked remarkably cool, and he didn't fidget. To Philip's satisfaction, the doctor Jack had seen in the spring had given a firm diagnosis of hypoglycemia, so Jack held only a glass of seltzer in his long, tapering fingers. Still, with his lean build, his groomed hair and angular jaw, he could have been at home in Monte Carlo. Ruth—his co-author, his dusky bedmate, at one time his self-proclaimed soul savior—had gone to Jamaica for an article on native sensuality and discovered some for herself. But along with a new diet, resigning his post had lifted Jack's spirits beyond a threat of heartbreak, and his new game, after all, was sex. A young dog still, he learned his tricks fast, and now he had sniffed out Didi Decker.

"I'm a better paddler than Ruth," she was saying.

"You're better at a lot of things. But it wouldn't be much cooler there. And you'd probably find a copperhead to bite you."

"There aren't any copperheads on the Colorado River."

"A moccasin, then."

"I don't think I want to go," Philip said. "Not now, anyway. Maybe in August." He was thinking of the relationship the three of them had had last year, aeons ago. Today felt as distant from that time as it would to a child, for whom each year meant an incomprehensible journey. He had still wanted something then, on the river. And, like one growing, he had seen the want filled and done away with.

"I'm hungry," said Didi. "Aren't those ready yet, Dad?"

"I guess so. The sun's probably broiled them."

"This guy at Berkeley told me the sun's farther away in summer."

"In the northern hemisphere's summer," Jack put in. "Which is why *no* great thinkers lived below the equator."

"A meaningless difference of two degrees Fahrenheit," countered Philip.

He served Jack and Didi, then gave himself a hamburger and a lump of potato salad. He wasn't hungry. They had eaten food like this on the patio almost every day, either for lunch while Emily was at day camp or in the evening, when the sun finally set. Jack almost always came, and when he came for dinner he stayed to play chess with Philip or watch TV with Didi before he spent the night in her room.

"I'm a lousy father," Philip said. "I ought to keep you at shooting distance from the house, Jack, and I ought to give Didi a lecture about the evils of older men, then take away her driving privileges. I shouldn't condone any of this."

"But you're no one to talk, and you know it," Didi said cheerfully.

"Seriously, I do worry about Emily. There's a lot for her to cope with as it is. I wish you two'd be more discreet."

Philip had come close to begging when he had asked Joan to send Emily back to Newhall; that is, he had asked softly and simply for her, and had ended with "please," and Joan had said, "You'd always be the main one anyway. But don't you fail her, Phil."

"Emily's fine," Jack said, biting into his hamburger. "What she needs is love and someone to watch her cartwheels, and you're giving her both. You dote on her besides."

"He spoils her, if you ask me," said Didi.

"So why not? Probably does him some good, too."

"Don't feel sorry for me, Jack, please. It makes you a bore," Philip warned. They were both bores, Jack and his daughter; they made him tired. He finished the beer and closed his eyes.

Where was she now? In a sailboat? On the beach? Did they have beaches in Wisconsin? He'd never been there. Why didn't she write, at least? A letter was not so difficult.

Joan had written after sending Emily down—an honest yet opaque epistle, devoid of rancor. At least he had not lost her goodwill. To ask her back would be an insult to her—better to wait. Even then, he suspected, she would not come. The Recovery Team could handle the condors without her for a while, she had written. There were only thirty left, after all. Away from the condor refuge, she had realized that the scheme was a doomed one anyway. The birds were committing suicide, and they would only survive, if they survived, as caged curiosities. She wasn't eager to hang around for the end, and she had no power to change the inevitable. There would be a boat leaving Point Reyes in August, to study migrations of seagoing birds for a full year. Relieved of Emily, Joan would be on it, at full salary. Philip was proud of her. *My wife.*

They were talking to him again. He opened his eyes. "What about the leave?" Didi was asking him. "Have you decided?"

"Sure—I'll take it. Why not?"

"But what'll you do, Phil?" asked Jack. He was at the grill, giving himself more meat.

"Work. I'll do what I was planning to do—take Emily to England, attend the symposium, write. I may come back in the spring, but not to teach. Didi can come too, if she wants. I can't see footing your bill, Jack, but nothing's stopping you, either. Write a bodice-buster set in Wales. Doing the dirty in the dungeon."

"Thanks, I like my lust modern-day."

"Are you sure Emily wants to go?" said Didi.

"Not at all sure. But I'm not leaving her here with the pair of you."

"Why go at all?"

"Because I can't stay here. What are you looking to do, Didi? Nurse me?" There was an edge to his voice, he heard it, throwing tension onto the sleepy patio. They were afraid of him, of what he'd say. They wanted to humor him. "I'm going inside," he said. "I've got work to do."

It was cooler in the house. Joan had always disdained air conditioning as wasteful and unhealthy, but fortunately the stone foundation provided natural insulation, and there was a constant draft. He puttered in the kitchen a minute, then gave the bonsai their exact quota of water—Didi had practically drowned them while he was away. Finally he washed up and headed for his cool, dark study. He really did mean to work. *Psychology* wanted an article on mental evolution and the philosophy of science. Can't be too academic, he thought. Must appeal to the intelligent masses. When he finished this he would draw back for a while—plumb his old ideas to the source. He would not publish anything more on the nature of the mind until he had it straight himself. He had begun to think he had something worthwhile to say, after all.

And he would live without a woman. What a difference that would make. Unless Annie came back. What was she doing now? Sketching costumes on some wide, screened porch with a slow overhead fan? Unless she returned, he preferred it that way. Work, that was what counted. And Emily. He had bought her a new bike, without training wheels, and he'd promised her a swimming pool by next summer. He read stories to her at night, or let her read to him. Didi was right, it was indulgent.

"Dad?" Didi stood at the door of the study, a loose shirt thrown over her swimsuit. "I hope I'm not bothering you."

"No, come in. I'm sorry I threw a kink into things, out there. Must be the heat."

"You were right to. We've been handling you with kid gloves, then pinching you where it hurts. I know you're annoyed by Jack."

"I'm used to him."

"Not to his being around all the time. I can't help it." She had pulled the footstool up to his desk and squatted on it, facing his knees. Her thick hair fell over her shoulders. "It won't last long, though, I don't think."

"Why not?"

"Well, first"—she hooked her index finger with her other thumb to tick off the reason—"he's not in love with me. He hangs out because he's in love with you."

"You too? Annie—" He stopped.

"Annie used to say that?"

"Yes. I don't know why Jack isn't allowed just to be attracted to young women of his choice. Even if it is cradle-snatching."

"Look who he chooses. And listen to what he says to them at intimate moments. Then you'd know."

"I'll pass." He reached down to lift a lock of hair out of her shirt collar. "And you?"

"That was the second reason." Her middle finger joined the index. "He's just something I've got to have for a little while."

"To hang out with," Philip tried to tease, "like Eugene at school?"

"To make the summer easier. At least till I sort some things out. There's this problem I have. . . ." She bent her head away, her voice trailing off.

"Yes? What problem?"

She shook her head, as if rejecting an offer, then turned her wide eyes on him. "You understand, don't you? It's not like I'm getting seduced by his charm or anything."

"You act as if you're being unfaithful to me."

"I feel like I am. Being with Jack feels unworthy."

"He's unworthy of you, probably, but you needn't live up to some ideal of me. You'll be twenty years old next week—I'm practically out of the picture."

"That's where you're wrong," Didi said. "You can't just get 'out of the picture,' like that. Not while you're in it, for me. And that goes for Jack, too." She had stood up and was walking around the room; she twisted her long hair into a bun, then let it fall.

Have you cut your hair? Philip asked Annie, to himself. *You were planning to.* She had said the sun would bleach it, and it had begun already to lighten in the desert—by now the fine curls might be close to blond. Had they been blond, last fall? He couldn't remember.

"Do you know how you're behaving?" he said to Didi. "Like

one of those daughters in a gothic southern novel, who sacrifices love and marriage to grow old caring for her dad."

"Who was a general in Lee's army but now lies paralyzed and irascible, a bullet lodged in his spine," Didi finished for him.

"Exactly."

"Well, I'm not that bad off." She leaned against the desk, close to him; he could smell her suntan oil.

"Nor am I."

"But we do need some time together, don't you think? You can't just close the book on me too, and transfer all your affection to Emily."

"You're jealous!"

"No, I'm not. But I'm not sure of you anymore. I want to be with you. I want to understand you."

"I'm not sure of myself either," he said. "And I don't entirely trust you."

"You have no reason to."

"Don't talk nonsense. Come to England, we'll work things out."

"Okay." She lifted her foot and rested it against his chair. "Jack will be gone by then, I promise."

"And stop promising junk like that. And stop taking care of me."

"Don't you want me to—just a little?"

"No." I sound like an old crank, he thought.

"All right, then—but we'll have fun together. Just wait. You'll forget her soon."

"I already have. Go on outside, now, I want to work."

"I love you, Philip," Didi said. She bent and put her arms around him, pressing her cheek to his face. He felt the oil on her warm skin. She rose quickly and went out.

She was a woman too, Philip realized as he wiped the oil from his cheek. What had he done to her? What had he done to all of them? And where was Annie now? She might be dancing, as she was always wanting to, with a whole crowd of young vacationers, like a celebrating tribe. Or curled up and reading fiction, her whole body folded into the depths of an armchair, while it poured Wisconsin rain outside, broken by summer lightning. Did she fit that body against another, at night? Did she know, now, the difference—the wanting she would always have, the terrible lack in things? Was she waiting, to be rescued?

He bent back over his work.